WOMENWITHOUT**MEN**

SHAHRNUSH PARSIPUR

WOMEN WITHOUT MEN

A NOVEL OF MODERN IRAN

Translated from the Persian by Kamran Talattof and Jocelyn Sharlet

AFTERWORD BY PERSIS M. KARIM

TRANSLATOR'S NOTE BY KAMRAN TALATTOF

THE FEMINIST PRESS
AT THE CITY UNIVERSITY OF NEW YORK
NEW YORK CITY

Published by the Feminist Press at the City University of New York
The Graduate Center, 365 Fifth Avenue, Suite 5406, New York, NY 10016
feministpress.org

Fourth printing September 2009

First Feminist Press edition, 2004
Originally published as *Zanan bedun mardan* in 1989 in Tehran, Iran. First English-language edition published in 1998 by Syracuse University Press, New York. This edition published by arrangement with Syracuse University Press and the author.

Library of Congress Cataloging-in-Publication Data
Parsipur, Shahrnush.
[Zanan bidun-i mardan. English]
Women without men / Shahrnush Parsipur ; translated from the Persian by Kamran Talattof and Jocelyn Sharlet ; afterword by Persis M. Karim.— 1st Feminist Press ed.
p. cm.
1. Women—Iran—Fiction. 2. Feminist fiction. I. Talattof, Kamran. II. Sharlet, Jocelyn. III. Title.
PK6561.P247Z3613 20
891'.5533—dc22 2003022954

This publication is made possible, in part, by public funds from the New York State Council on the Arts and the National Endowment for the Arts. The Feminist Press would also like to thank Elisabeth Driscoll, Helene D. Goldfarb, Barbara Grossman, Dorothy O. Helly, Nancy Hoffman, Florence Howe, Marjorie Lightman, Betty Prashker, and Marilyn Reznick for their generosity.

Contents

Mahdokht 1
Faizeh 13
Munis 29
Mrs. Farrokhlaqa Sadraldivan Golchehreh 53
Zarrinkolah 71
Two Girls on the Road 78
Farrokhlaqa's Garden 82
The Garden 101
Mahdokht 120
Faizeh 123
Munis 127
Farrokhlaqa Sadraldivan Golchehreh 129
Zarrinkolah 131

Afterword by Persis M. Karim 133
Translating Context: A Translator's Note
by Kamran Talattof 175

Mahdokht

The deep green garden, its walls plastered with mud and hay, faced the river, with the village behind it. The side by the river had no wall; the river was the border. It was a garden of sour and sweet cherries. In the garden was a house, half village house, half city house, with three rooms and a pool in front that was full of scum and frogs. The area around the pool was paved with pebbles, with a few willows nearby. In the afternoon, the light green reflection of the willows was in a silent battle with the dark green of the pool. This always troubled Mahdokht, for she could not tolerate any conflict. She was a simple woman, and wished that everyone could get along, even the myriad greens of the world.

"Such a tranquil color, but still. . . ," she thought.

A long bench sat under one of the trees at the edge of the pool. Because of the slime, there was always the possibility that it would slide and fall completely into the pool. On this bench Mahdokht would sit and watch the conflicts among the water and the willow's reflection, and the blue of the sky, which in the afternoon more than at any other time imposed itself on this gathering of shades of green, and which seemed to Mahdokht to be the divine judge between them.

In the winter, Mahdokht knit or thought about studying French or taking a trip, because in the winter one could breathe the clear, chill air, whereas in the summer, everything seemed to be finished. For summer was full of smoke and swirling clouds of dust from passing cars and pedestrians, and the sadness of windows in the burning sun.

"Damn these people, why don't they understand that the windows can't cure the pain of this country," she thought.

She had been forced to accept her older brother Hoshang's invitation to come to the garden and endure the noise of the children, who shouted and ate cherries all day, and then had the runs and ate yoghurt all night.

"The yoghurt is from the village."

"Yes, it's excellent."

The children were always cold and pale, even though they ate more than they needed, so that they could sprout up, as their mother would say.

Before, when she was a teacher, Mr. Ehteshami would say, "Miss Parhani, please put this notebook over there . . . Miss Parhani, ring the bell . . . Miss Parhani, say something to this Soghra, I have no idea what she wants . . . " Mr. Ehteshami liked for her to be the disciplinarian. It wasn't so bad. But one day Mr. Ehteshami said, "Miss Parhani, would you like to go to the movies with me tonight? There's a good movie showing."

Mahdokht turned pale. She did not know how to respond to this insult. What was this guy thinking? Who did he think she was? What did he really want? Now she understood why the other female teachers would stop smiling when Mr. Ehteshami spoke to her. They were assuming something, but they were wrong to think anything. Now she would show them all who she was. Mahdokht didn't go to school. The following year, when she heard that Mr. Ehteshami had married Miss Ata'i, the history teacher, she felt her heart contract.

"The problem is that dear father has left a lot of money."

That's the way it was. The following year, she spent the whole winter knitting. She knitted for Hoshang's first two children, who had just begun to walk. Ten years later, she was knitting for five children. "It's not clear why they have so many kids."

Hoshang would say, "It's out of my control. I like children, what can I do."

"Well, what can he do, really," she thought.

She had recently seen a movie with Julie Andrews. Her fiancé was an Austrian with seven children that he sent running this way and that with his whistle. In the end he married Julie. Of course, at first, Julie was going to go home and become a nun, but then she decided to marry the Austrian, since she was carrying his eighth child. That seemed like the best thing to do, especially because the Germans were coming and everything was happening fast.

"I am just like Julie," she thought.

She was right. She was like Julie. If she saw an ant with a broken leg, she would cry her eyes out. She had fed the starving stray dogs four times, and had given her new overcoat to the school custodian. When she was a teacher, she had participated in a charitable program by bringing several kilos of sweets to an orphanage.

"Such nice children," she thought.

She wouldn't have minded having some of them as her own. What was wrong with that? They would always have clean clothes to wear, and the snot would not run down their faces, and they would never pronounce the word "toilet" in such a crude way.

"What would become of them?"

Her question was a hard one. The government would sometimes announce on the radio or on television that something must be done about the orphans.

Both the government and Mahdokht were worried about the children. If only Mahdokht had a thousand hands and could knit five hundred sweaters a week. Every two hands could knit one sweater, so that would make five hundred sweaters.

But a person cannot have a thousand hands, especially Mahdokht, who liked the winter and liked to go for walks in the afternoon. Besides, it would take at least five hours just to put a thousand gloves on.

"No, with five hundred of my hands I could put gloves on the other five hundred. Three minutes at the most."

These are not the problems. They will eventually be solved. It's the government's responsibility, they should open a factory to knit sweaters.

Mahdokht wiggled her feet in the water of the pool.

The first day that she came to the garden she went to the riverbank and stood in the water. The icy water froze her feet so that she had to step out quickly. She could have caught cold. After she put her shoes back on, she went over to the greenhouse. The door to the greenhouse was open, and the humid air inside was warmer than summer air. Years ago Mr. Ehteshami had said that breathing the humid air of the greenhouse during the day was the best thing you could do, because all the flowers produce oxygen. He said this even though at that time they had taken all the flowers from the greenhouse and put them in the garden. Mahdokht walked along the narrow aisle in the greenhouse looking at the dusty windows. She heard the sound of breathing and struggling, something burning and hot, the smell of bodies.

Mahdokht's heart stopped. The girl, Fatemeh, at fifteen like a worldly woman, was at the end of the greenhouse with Yadallah, the gardener. With his bald head and oozing eyes, it was difficult to look at him.

The world around her went dark, and her legs began to tremble. She involuntarily clutched the edge of a table. But she could not take her eyes off them. She looked and looked until they saw her. The guy had begun to whimper. He wanted to escape but he couldn't. He was mindlessly beating the girl. The girl extended her hand toward Mahdokht. Mahdokht ran out of the greenhouse. She didn't know what to do. She headed for the pool in a daze, and wanted to throw up. She washed her hands and sat on the bench.

"What can I do?"

She thought about going to Hoshang and his wife and telling all. The girl was under their supervision.

"A little girl of fifteen—how awful . . . "

Hoshang would certainly give the girl a severe beating. Then they would let her go. Fatemeh's brothers would surely kill her.

"What can I do?"

She would quickly pack her bags and return to Tehran. At least that would be better than this anxiety.

"So what to do?"

She was paralyzed, but she felt compelled to return fearfully to the greenhouse. The girl stumbled out with her chador on inside out. Her face was red and scratched.

"Madam," she said, throwing herself at Mahdokht's feet.

"She is whimpering like a dog," Mahdokht thought. "Go away, you filthy thing."

"No, madam, in the name of God, may I die for you. May I be your sacrifice."

"Shut up, step aside."

"In the name of God, may I be your sacrifice. If you tell my mother she'll kill me."

"Who said I wanted to tell?"

"By God, he wants to marry me. Tomorrow he's supposed to tell the master."

Mahdokht had to promise not to tell just to get the girl to leave her alone. When the girl's hands touched Mahdokht's feet, she felt disgusted. The girl walked back to the greenhouse, crestfallen. Mahdokht drew a deep breath. She felt an urge to cry.

Now three months had passed and the summer would be over in a few days. That day they would all go back to the city and no one would ever find out why Yadallah the gardener left so abruptly. Hoshang said, "It's strange, he himself said a hundred times that he wouldn't leave."

They had to hire another caretaker for the garden so that it wouldn't be vandalized during the winter. Without a caretaker, anyone could put four benches by the river and rent them out for thirty tomans a day to groups of men who wanted to hang out. Hoshang said this and everyone believed him.

The sound of Fatemeh's shrill laughter came from the end of the garden. She had taken the children out to play, and God only knew what kind of games she was teaching them. Mahdokht paced back and forth in her room, beating the door and walls with her fists. She was worried about the children.

"I hope she's pregnant so that they kill her," she thought.

It would be good if she were pregnant. All her

brothers would descend on her and beat her to death. How good that would be. Then the children would not be corrupted.

"My virginity is like a tree," she thought suddenly.

She had to look in a mirror. She had to see her face.

"Maybe that's why I am green."

Her face was yellowish green. There were shadows under her eyes and the veins showed on her forehead.

Mr. Ehteshami had said, "How cold you are, like ice."

Now she thought, "Not like ice. I am a tree."

She could plant herself in the ground.

"I'm not a seed, I'm a tree. I must plant myself."

How could she tell this to Hoshang? She wanted to say, dear brother, let's sit down and have a friendly talk. As you know, the factories knit sweaters. But if she said this, she would have to explain about the thousand hands. She couldn't explain about the hands. It was impossible for Hoshang to understand this. How could she say, when thousands of factories knit sweaters, there was no need for her to knit.

Well, there was no alternative. Mahdokht decided to stay in the garden and plant herself at the beginning of winter. She had to ask the gardeners what was the best time for planting. She didn't know, but it wasn't important. She would stay and plant herself. Perhaps she would turn into a tree. She wanted to grow on the riverbank with leaves greener than the slime, and fight the battle of shades of green in the pool. If she became a tree, she would sprout new leaves. She would be covered with new leaves. She would give her new leaves to the wind, a garden full of Mahdokhts. They would have to cut down all the sour and sweet cherry trees so that Mahdokht could grow. Mahdokht would grow.

She would become thousands and thousands of branches. She would cover the entire world. Americans would buy her shoots and take them to California. They would call the forest of Mahdokht the forest of Mahdekat. Gradually they would pronounce her name so many times until it would become Maduk in some places and Maaduk in others. Then four hundred years later the linguists, with their veins standing out in their foreheads like twigs, would debate over her and prove that the two words come from the root Madeek which is of African origin. Then the biologists would object that a tree that grows in cold climates could not grow in Africa.

Mahdokht banged her head on the wall again and again until she broke into tears. Between sobs she thought that this year she would definitely take a trip to Africa. She would go to Africa so that she could grow. She wanted to be a tree in a warm climate. She wanted to, and it is always desire that drives one to madness.

Faizeh

At four o'clock in the afternoon on the twenty-fifth of August, 1953, after days of hesitation, Faizeh made a decision. Silence no longer had any meaning. Had she waited longer, everything would have fallen apart. She had to go and defend her rights.

In spite of all the power that was moving in her, it took her an hour to get dressed. She slowly pulled on her socks and put on a linen skirt and blouse. While she got dressed she thought for a moment that Amir might be there. The thought of his being there made her entire body burning hot. If Amir was there she certainly would not be comfortable saying all the things that she wanted to say. She would not be able to speak. She would have to keep everything inside, and once again be plagued by insecurity. Every time she wanted to speak something happened, followed by hesitation and indecision, waffling and wavering.

As she stood before the mirror powdering her face, she said to herself, I am getting old. Twenty-eight years and two months of her life gone. Of course, she wasn't really old, just weak.

She put her shoes on, picked up her purse, and went down the stairs. Grandma was sitting on the bench in the courtyard looking at the pool. The tapping of Faizeh's heels distracted her. She asked, "Are you going out?"

"Yes!"

"Not a good idea. There are crowds everywhere."

The neighbor's radio was on and its noise reached the courtyard. Faizeh hesitated. Grandma was right. Grandma said, "At least put your chador on."

Faizeh went back upstairs without a word. She pulled her funeral chador out from under a pile of clothes and put it on in front of the mirror. There were large creases in the soft fabric. If Amir was there he would surely tease her. She liked Amir's teasing, but not about this kind of thing. It was all right for him to tease her about not having a husband, but it would be bad if he teased her about the chador. She might cry, and it was not good to cry in front of

Amir. At any rate there was no alternative. She went back down the stairs, this time with the chador.

Grandma didn't talk much anymore. It had been a long time since she told people what to do.

She went out to the alley. Noise came from far away. She found a taxi immediately, got in, and said, "Sezavar."

The driver looked at her in the rearview mirror. As he pulled away from the curb, he said, "Aren't you afraid? It's really crowded."

"I have no choice."

The driver said, "I have to take the long way around. I can't take the main road. It's dangerous."

"That's fine."

The driver was following the back streets. At one intersection there was a small traffic jam. Someone was standing in the street ordering the cars to stop. Suddenly the man who was in the middle of the street jumped onto the sidewalk. He was moving quickly. Someone was following him. The man turned into an alley and disappeared. The cars started to move quickly.

Another man jumped onto the back of Faizeh's taxi

and banged on the window with a knife. Faizeh didn't look at him. She put her head down on her knees and for a moment regretted coming out. The driver slammed on the brakes, and Faizeh's head hit the front seat. Then he hit the accelerator, and her body was jerked backward. The man had been thrown off the back of the taxi. The driver said, "I told you it was dangerous. I'm going to call it a day."

Faizeh didn't answer. The driver said, "Damn it! I should have known better. My wife told me a dozen times not to go out."

Faizeh didn't answer. She didn't like the way the man kept staring at her in the rearview mirror. She wanted to get out of the taxi as soon as possible.

Finally they arrived. She paid the driver, but she was so disgusted at touching his hand that she didn't wait for the change.

The uproar could still be heard from afar. Faizeh rang the bell. For two minutes she waited uncomfortably until Alia opened the door. She looked sleepy. Faizeh said, "You're still sleeping? God."

Alia greeted her and stepped aside to let Faizeh in. Faizeh asked, "Is Munis here?"

"Yes, she is."

"Where is she?"

"She should be in the living room."

Faizeh headed toward the living room. With her first step she thought, she's here. With the second step she thought, she's not here. And so on until she reached the door. It was the fifth step. She thought, she's here, and opened the door. Munis was sitting alone in front of the radio, listening attentively. Amir was not there. Faizeh thought, he must be upstairs sleeping.

Munis' face lit up. "Honey, how are you? God, it's been ages," she said, standing up slowly. She turned down the radio.

"Where've you been? We never hear from you."

The women kissed and fussed over each other and then sat down by the radio. Faizeh asked, "Are you alone?"

"Yes, I am. They all went to Mashhad."

"So why didn't you tell me?"

"They just left two days ago."

"Well, what about Amir?"

"He's not here. He's at work."

"How can anybody work in this chaos?"

"When he goes out he says he's going to work. How should I know?"

"Go figure!"

"I'm glad you're here."

"Don't mention it."

"No, really. Want some tea?"

"If it's not any trouble."

Munis got up and Faizeh turned off the radio. The radio could have prevented them from talking. She was gone longer than necessary and then came back and sat down across from Faizeh without a word.

Faizeh had read somewhere that people with round faces are stupid. When she read that, she had quickly run to look in the mirror. She knew that her face wasn't round. They had told her many times that she was horse-faced. Grandma had said that so many times, in that stinging tone of hers. She had run to look at herself and made sure that she could not be one of the stupid people.

After that she got into the habit of evaluating faces. Amir had a square face with a square jaw, but Munis had a round face. Very round. Something between a moon and an egg, so that for years Faizeh thought Munis was stupid, even though she was ten years older. In spite of this, there was something about Munis that kept their friendship going.

Only after two years did Amir appear. She was seeing Munis now for her own sake and also for Amir's sake. If Munis had had a longer face, it would have occurred to her to arrange a marriage between Faizeh and Amir. Faizeh had often thought, poor girl, why is her face so round?

Alia brought the tea. As they drank it Munis glanced at the radio. Although she was older and in her own house, she didn't dare turn it back on. She asked, "Is there a riot outside?"

"Yes, it's really bad."

"Amir told me not to go out. He said it's crazy out there."

"He's right. Someone jumped onto the back of my taxi." After a moment, she asked "Have you seen Parvin lately?"

"Not for about a month."

"Why not?"

"Her son was sick. She said he had the measles, and that it was better not to have visitors so that the germs wouldn't spread all over the place."

"In that case it's good that you didn't see her."

Munis looked at Faizeh out of the corner of her eye. Faizeh was waiting for her to say something so that she could continue, but the woman just sat there staring at the flowers in the carpet.

Faizeh began again, "I swear I have never seen such a shameless person in my life." Munis looked up in surprise.

"Why?"

It was an innocent question, but Faizeh thought, God, if only she didn't have such a round face.

"She's so vile. It's horrible to find that out after ten or fifteen years of friendship. She's a good woman on the surface. But she has no class at all. There is nothing she won't do."

Munis looked bewildered. "What does she want to do? Does she want to get divorced?"

"No, the poor thing. She's tried everything but divorce. She's the worst. My poor brother."

Munis was curious. She was trying to understand Parvin's shamelessness, but she couldn't figure it out. She had mostly seen the woman at Faizeh's house or at parties and funerals. They had a simple friendship, and Munis had never found anything not to like.

Munis looked at Faizeh, waiting for her to explain why Parvin was shameless. Faizeh started to cry. Her tears were reflected in Munis's eyes, and then Munis started to cry too. It was always like this. Whenever somebody cried Munis cried too, without understanding why. Munis said, "Don't cry. For God's sake, don't cry. What's wrong?"

Faizeh looked for a tissue but couldn't find one. She wiped her eyes with a corner of the chador that was spread around her.

"Do you know how nice I was to her? Do you think she would have been so happy if I wasn't there for her? It was just last year that she and my brother separated. It was her own fault. That stupid woman packed her bags and went to her mother's house. A woman with an ounce of dignity would never do such a thing. You know who fixed things up between them? Me. I made a dinner that the entire city still remembers. I went to Mirkhavand the butcher and tipped him so that he would give me the best cuts of meat. I made eggplant. I made lamb and rice. And grilled chicken—such grilled chicken! Marinated in lemon juice, mint, herbs, and spices. It took me an hour and a half to grill it in the yard. I made yoghurt and spinach. You think there were tomatoes to be had? I went down to the market and found them. I had the colonial officer's assistant buy vodka so that I could pour it down her father's throat."

Faizeh bit her lip. Bitterness welled up inside of her.

"Then what?"

"What do you think? I arranged another wedding. I sent her back to my brother's house. Then two months later the bitch wanted to repay me. She actually wanted to ruin me. One night she had a party. The filthy woman made European food. She threw a few pieces of leather on a platter and called it steak. As if we were dogs. As if we had no sense of taste. From then on I knew that she wanted war. And I thought, I will give you a war that you will never forget."

"She never told me that she wanted a war."

"What would she say? What could she say? She wants to be better than me. All my life, everyone who has eaten Faizeh's cooking has said it's delicious. Now this little bitch wants to declare war?"

"I see."

"So I went and bought a cookbook. If a person can make lamb and rice, she can make rubber steak. I learned it all.

"Of course you learned. There's nothing to it. Every day on the radio they tell how to make it."

"That's what I wanted to prove. So I gave another dinner party."

"When?"

"A month ago. I told them all to come for European food. I went to Mirkhavand's and tipped him and bought eight pieces of filet mignon, one per person. I bought French peas, green beans, importedtomatoes, and potatoes. I made beans and rice with salad. I made yoghurt and spinach. Honey, I made a sauce for those steaks like nothing you've ever tasted. I went to the market and bought the biggest peaches and nectarines and sweet and sour cherries. I had the colonial officer's assistant buy vodka. I poured the vodka in a pitcher and put the pitcher on ice in Grandma's crystal bowl."

Munis looked at Faizeh with admiration. "Why did you do that?"

Faizeh smiled. "So that the vodka would stay cool."

"Wow!"

"If only you could have seen it."

"So why didn't you invite me?"

"Well, Amir was in Shiraz. I didn't think you'd want to go home alone at night."

"Oh."

"Let me tell you, they ate it and said it was delicious. They were beside themselves. That woman was about to die of envy."

"Parvin?"

"Who do you think? You know what she did?"

"No."

"She had the nerve to call me 'Fawzi honey'. The filthy thing called me 'Fawzi honey'. It's too much work for her to open her mouth and say Faizeh. She said, 'Fawzi honey, I have to tell you something. You don't put sauce on filet mignon.' She said it loud enough for all the neighbors to hear."

"Wow."

"You can't imagine how I felt. I said, who says you can't put sauce on filet mignon? She said she heard it on the radio. I said, but I read about it in a book. She said that she had read about it in a book too. I said her book must have been wrong. Too bad my brother interfered. He said, 'Whether they use sauce or not, this is delicious.' The bitch got all choked up when my brother defended me. She was all choked up the whole night."

Munis had become so intrigued with the story that Faizeh felt compelled to spice it up a bit. She said, "So then, when the men went out to the terrace, she stayed inside like she wanted to help me clean up."

Faizeh fell silent and bit her nails. She couldn't stand to think of it. Tears rolled down her cheeks. Munis said, "For God's sake, please don't cry."

Munis cried too. Faizeh said, "When the table was cleared, that woman said, 'A woman who spends half her life making out with Farid in the hall should do something about her curtain of virginity, not waste all her time cooking.'" Tears poured down Faizeh's face onto her skirt.

Munis was bewildered and crying. She asked, "Who's Farid?"

"Her brother, the bastard. The piece of shit. Like a piece of filth that didn't get flushed. Then me and Farid . . . I saw red. First I thought of slapping her so hard upside the head that her eardrum would break. Too bad my brother was there. Then I thought, I have to fight fire with fire. I said, 'First of all, the only one who messes around with your brother in the hall is the angel of death, because with that face only the angel of death would have him. Second, virginity is not a curtain, it's a hole. You've had three kids and you still don't know that it's a hole, not a curtain. And then you spread rumors about people.'"

Munis had stopped crying. She was just staring at Faizeh. Faizeh said, "I told her, if she opened her filthy mouth again, I would tear her into a hundred pieces. At least the bitch was afraid of my brother. She was dead silent."

Munis silently stared at the flowers in the carpet. As Faizeh wiped away her tears, she carefully followed the changes in Munis's face. She said, "She's a snake. She won't slither away until she has bitten someone. Now she'll go around badmouthing me. So what? A person with a clean account doesn't fear the auditor. She made me so angry that I wanted to go to Mrs. Mahjabin to get a certificate of virginity and frame it on the wall for her jealous eyes to see.

Munis was still staring at the flowers in the carpet. Then she said, "Virginity is a curtain, my mother says. If a girl jumps down from a height she'll damage her virginity. It's a curtain, it can be torn."

"What are you talking about? It's a hole. It's narrow, and then it becomes wide."

"Oh!"

Munis turned pale. Faizeh looked at her and asked, "Is something wrong?"

"No, nothing. But it must be a curtain."

"No. I read about it in a book. I read a lot. It's a hole."

Amir arrived as Alia entered with a bowl of fruit. Faizeh greeted him modestly. The squarely built man acknowledged them and sat down in an armchair across the room. He said, "It's really crazy out there. Don't go out." Then he noticed that the girls' eyes were red. He asked, "Is something wrong?"

Munis said, "No."

Amir's kind look disappeared. "I said, is something wrong?"

Faizeh said, "We've been talking things over."

"So why are you crying?"

"Well, we're women."

Amir smiled coldly.

Faizeh said, "I have to go."

Amir said, "Where to? It's crazy out there."

"I have to go, it's getting late."

Amir wanted to tell her to stay the night. But it was not possible. Her family would worry. He said,

"I'll take you home. It's been a pleasure to have you here. But it's not a day for a woman to go out alone."

"It's not that bad, Amir."

He frowned. "It doesn't make sense for a woman to go out in the first place. Home is for women, the outside world for men."

Faizeh didn't answer. There was no point in debating with Amir. Fruit ripens by itself.

She was no longer worried about Parvin. There was nothing left for the woman to do to her.

Amir stood up to take her home before nightfall. The girl was happy to be alone with him. She said, "It's not dangerous if we take back streets. That's what the driver said."

Munis

At four o'clock in the afternoon on the twenty-seventh day of August, 1953, Munis was standing on the roof looking down at the street. It had been exactly fifty-six hours since she had last slept. Amir had said that she must not go out.

The street was crowded, full of people running around. Trucks full of people and tanks passed by, and the sound of machine-gun fire came from afar.

Munis thought about how for thirty-eight years she had been looking out the window at the little garden, assuming that virginity was a curtain. When she was eight years old, they had told her that God would never forgive a girl who lost her virginity. Now it had been three days and two nights since she found out that virginity is a hole, not a curtain. Something inside of her had broken. She was filled with a cold rage. She recalled how, when she was a child, she used to gaze longingly at the trees, wishing that just once she could climb one. But she never had, out of fear for her virginity. She didn't know why her legs felt ice-cold up to her knees. She said, "I'll take revenge!"

A man turned into an alley. He was clutching his chest and staggering along. He took a few steps forward and then fell headfirst into the gutter, which was filled with running water. She couldn't see his head anymore, but his legs were sticking out of the gutter. Munis closed her eyes and bent forward. Five seconds later she was lying flat on her back on the alley pavement. But her eyes were still open, looking up at the clear blue sky.

At first Munis was dead. Or perhaps she was thinking that she was dead. For a while she lay on her back on the alley pavement with her eyes open. Little by little the light blue sky turned black. Tears rolled down her face. She raised her right hand and wiped her eyes. Then she stood up. Her body felt sore and extremely weak.

A man was lying in the gutter with his feet sticking out. Munis went over to the man in a daze. His face was turned toward the sky and his eyes were open. Munis asked, "Are you all right?"

The man said, "I'm dead."

"Can I help you?"

"The best thing is for you to go away. You might get into trouble."

"Why?"

"Can't you hear the uproar? They're settling all the scores."

"So what are you doing here?"

"Ma'am, I told you, I'm dead."

"If I take care of you now, maybe you'll get better."

"No, I don't think so. It's too late for that. There's a French movie called, 'It's too late'. I am now at that stage—it's too late."

Munis was terribly distressed. She said, "But maybe . . ."

The man got angry. "I said go away! This is insane."

Then Munis left and spent a month walking the streets. At first the streets were crowded. People were busy beating and killing each other. Gradually the streets became empty, and people went home, thinking things over and feeling regret. Some went to prison. Some were happy, drinking vodka and wine and laughing at parties. The not-so-young girl didn't go to parties, but she passed by the windows where the parties were and listened to the laughter inside. At night nobody went out because of the curfew.

Eventually Munis began to walk past the bookstores across from the university. On several days she stood there modestly and looked at the covers of the books, not allowing herself to read the titles. Gradually her fear disappeared and she began to read the titles. Finally, one day, not in the window of a bookseller but in one of the stalls in the street, the title of a book caught her eye: *The Secret of Sexual Satisfaction or How to Know Our Bodies*.

For twelve days Munis passed by the bookstall stealing looks at the title of the book. On the thirteenth day she got up the nerve to approach the bookstall.

"How much is this one?"

"Five tomans."

Munis bought the book and went off to a quiet street. She sat under a tree and began to read the book. She read it cover to cover and read it again and again, until three days had passed.

On the third day she looked up. The trees and sunshine and streets all had new meanings for her. She had grown up.

She threw the book in the gutter and began to walk home.

She arrived home at sunset. Alia opened the door. At the sight of Munis, Alia screamed and passed out. Munis helped her up and asked, "Alia, what's wrong?"

As she came to she said, "Ma'am, we were worried sick about you. For a month your parents and your brother have been combing the city and the countryside looking high and low for you, crying their eyes out. Ma'am, where have you been, what have you been doing?"

Munis didn't answer. She just shook her head and smiled enigmatically. Finally she said, "Alia dear, I'm not the same person that I was before. Now I know a lot."

Then she calmly went to the living room, sat down in a corner, and began to think. After a little while,

Amir appeared in the threshold, looking anxious and upset.

"Where have you been, you shameless woman?"

Munis smiled sweetly. She saw no reason to be angry. Amir said, "You have destroyed our family's reputation. Now everybody and their cousin knows that you are ruined."

"I simply went for a little walk with your permission."

"I told you not to go out during the riot, you shameless woman." As he said this he took off his belt and began to beat Munis. She did not know why he was beating her. After a while she asked, "Amir, why are you doing this? Are you out of your mind?"

Upon hearing this Amir saw red. He took the fruit knife from the lunch table and stabbed Munis in the chest.

Munis said good-bye to life for the second time.

Hearing the shouting, Alia entered the room. When she saw Munis's bloody body and the bloody knife in Amir's right hand, she screamed and passed out. Amir was confused and frightened. For a few moments he looked in wonder at the knife and then put it on the edge of the table. Then he changed his mind, picked up the knife, pulled a handkerchief out of his pocket, wiped the fingerprints off the handle, and put the knife back on the table.

At that moment the doorbell rang. Amir went to the door. It was his parents.

"We went to three police stations, but they haven't found her yet."

They entered the living room. First they saw Alia. Then Munis. For a moment they looked at each other in bewilderment. Then they both cried out and fainted.

Amir was standing there helplessly looking at the four bodies on the floor. He said to himself, "God, what should I do?"

He sat on the edge of a chair and looked at the horrible sight. Finally he couldn't take it anymore and broke down crying. He cried for a while. He wiped his face with his handkerchief and then discovered that it was covered with blood.

His entire body trembling, Amir threw the handkerchief down on the table and continued to stare in astonishment at the bodies. None of them showed any sign of gaining consciousness. Everything was up to him.

The doorbell rang.

Amir's heart pounded like a clock striking. As he stood up, he said, "God help me."

They had notified several police stations about Munis, and every day at least five police officers would stop by the house and ring the bell.

Amir went to the door and jerked it open. It was Faizeh. At first when Amir's face was in the dark, and she couldn't see it clearly, she said, "Hello!"

Then she saw his face and said, "Good God!"

She leaned against the wall. Amir said, "For God's sake, don't you go and faint too."

Faizeh stood there looking fearfully at Amir's face, and said shakily, "I've come to get news about Munis."

Amir pointed toward the living room. The girl went to the room and opened the door. Amir remained in the hall. She came out looking pale.

"You killed them?"

"Only Munis."

"What are you going to do now?"

"I don't know."

As he said this he squatted down against the wall like a bug and broke down sobbing. At this point Faizeh felt that the hand of fate had finally showed her the way. She took off her chador, crumpled it up and threw it in a corner, and squatted down in front of Amir. She said, "You're a man! You can't cry. What are you crying for? You're a brother, you upheld your family's honor. You killed her? You did the right thing. Why not? A girl who disappears for a month is as good as dead. A girl doesn't do such a thing. You really did the right thing. Good for you, I would have done the same thing. Your mother raised you well."

As she said this, she took a handkerchief from between her breasts and gave it to him.

Amir grew quiet and blew his nose with the handkerchief. He was waiting for consolation, and it was as if it had fallen from the sky. At the same time, he was thinking about how ugly a woman looks squatting on the floor, pulling a handkerchief from between her breasts. While she was sitting like that her underwear showed. Amir thought that if she were his sister, he would kill her too. But of course she was not his sister, and it was none of his business. Also, she was there for him at a crucial time. Finally Amir sighed and asked, "So what do you think we should do?"

"It's very simple. It's been a month since the girl disappeared, right?"

"Yes."

"We'll bury her in the garden. No one will know. Many people disappear and the detectives are busy. No one is going to come to your house to ask about her." This seemed logical to Amir. They went out to the dark yard, and with a pick and shovel dug a three-foot-deep grave in the garden. Then they went back to the living room.

Amir's parents and Alia were still unconscious. The man and the woman picked up Munis's body, carried it out to the garden, and put it in the hole. They filled the hole and packed the dirt down with the shovel. Then they went back inside and began to clean up the blood.

After they had finished cleaning, Amir's parents and Alia gradually regained consciousness. The shock of what had happened had caused them to forget the events of the past two or three hours. Only Alia had a vague recollection of having seen a dead body, but because she was a poor servant, she did not dare to say so, especially because there was a rumor that Munis had a double whom the neighbors had seen walking along the edge of the roof by night and opening mosquito nets to gaze impudently upon the people inside. So Alia kept quiet.

Amir's mother, upon seeing Faizeh, glowed with happiness.

"Faizeh dear, how are you? It's been a long time."

"No, I'm always here bothering you."

"What do you mean? You're like a daughter to me."

"I just stopped by to ask about poor Munis. To find out whether she's been found or not." Amir's mother sighed and said, "My poor child still has not been found! She'll be found, God willing."

Faizeh said, "Well, I won't bother you anymore. For God's sake, let me know as soon as she is found."

The mother said, "You think we're going to let you go? Absolutely not. You must stay for dinner. Alia, run into the kitchen."

"No, ma'am. If you'll excuse me, I won't bother you anymore."

"Absolutely not."

So Faizeh stayed for dinner, and Alia went into the kitchen.

Faizeh was in the habit of singing love songs while making dinner. In these songs, the lover lamented that if he were literate he would pick up a pen and write a letter to his distant beloved and explain the things that he could not articulate.

Finally they ate dinner. After dinner Amir volunteered to take Faizeh home. On the way he was quiet and in shock. The girl dared to hold his hand and caress it. Finally she threw caution to the wind and said, "Now, after this incident, you must get married as soon as possible so that people will forget about Munis. Anyway, you need a partner in life who can take care of you."

"You're right."

A few days later Amir said to his mother, "Mother!"

"Yes, my dear!"

Amir was sitting on the edge of a chair and seemed a bit tense.

"Mother dear, I really shouldn't be speaking of such things right now. But for some time I've been thinking and have concluded that I need a wife who can be my partner in life and take care of me."

His mother said, "Wonderful! What could be better. Of course your sister, may she rest in peace, has not been found yet. It would be nice if she could be here for this blessed occasion. Well, what can be done. Anyway, God willing, when do you intend to get married, and where will the ceremony be?"

Amir coughed with embarrassment, and said, "Of course we must first make the proposal."

His mother asked in surprise, "You're not going to marry Faizeh?"

"No, Mother. I will marry the daughter of Hajj Mohammad Sorkhchehreh. She's eighteen years old, very beautiful, soft and quiet, modest, shy, kind, diligent, hard-working, dignified, chaste, elegant, and neat. She wears a chador, always looks down when she's in the street, and blushes constantly. You must do me the favor of asking her hand in marriage for me."

"Amir, my dear. You are two years older than your late sister, and forty sweet years of your life have passed. During this time you have not married because you wanted to protect and take care of your sister. Now why do you want an eighteen-year-old? Haven't you heard the saying that when you take a young wife, you take her for your neighbor? You know that in such a case you may find yourself in an embarrassing situation?"

Amir thought a little bit and then said, "Mother dear, you know the saying that you have to have pity for a woman who reaches twenty. I must marry a girl younger than twenty. Also, it's obvious from her appearance that she won't be unchaste. So today you must dress up and go ask for her hand in marriage."

That evening, his mother put on her best dress and her chador, and together with Amir went to make the proposal. They exchanged greetings with the girl's family. The girl, with her head scarf tied on tight and wearing thick stockings, modestly brought tea to the guests.

Amir's mother liked the bride, and the bride liked her. The groom's family liked the bride's family, and the bride's family liked the groom's family. They agreed to have the wedding on the following Wednesday, because the holy months were coming up, which would mean a delay. The payment in case of divorce was set at fifteen thousand tomans, and it was decided that Amir would bring a mirror and candelabra, and that the wedding would be held in the Hajji's yard because it was more spacious and beautiful.

Then the mother and son happily returned home and told Alia all about it. Alia nodded wisely and smiled enigmatically and at the first opportunity put on her chador and went to tell Faizeh the news. The girl hit her head against the wall for a while. Then she hit the window with her fist, breaking the glass and wounding her hand. Taking Alia's advice, she put on her chador and they went to the shrine of Shah Abdulazim, where she lit twelve candles and vowed to sacrifice a fat sheep if the wedding didn't take place. Then they went to Darvazeh Ghar to see Mirza Manaqebi, from whom she obtained a love-destroying talisman.

From there they went to a village to see Madam Baji, who had a pure soul and an old book with which she told fortunes. She scrutinized Faizeh, opened the book, and said, "The recipient of the fortune is a girl who is not too tall and not too short, not too fat and not too thin. She has a nice olive complexion, a square face, small eyes, and ruby-red lips." Faizeh was surprised at how accurate the book was. Madam Baji continued, "She is sad, and her sadness is the sadness of love. God will help her." Faizeh nodded her head vigorously. At that moment, she loved Madam Baji as much as her mother. The tiny old woman said, "The way to overcome this love is for the girl to walk seven steps toward Mecca and seven steps back, barefoot, each night for seven nights, saying with each step, 'O God, save me from the evil and temptation of Satan.' Then she should wash her feet with water and keep her feet outside the covers when she goes to sleep."

Faizeh said, "Madam Baji, I am in love. I want to capture the heart of the man I love. Give me a talisman that will make him want me."

Madam Baji was very old. She laughed, and said, "My dear girl, nothing can be kept by force. You must fight this love. How appropriate is the saying, 'How good it is when love comes to two heads, for love that comes to one head is a headache.'"

Faizeh threw a coin on the carpet and left. When she was gone Madam Baji laughed. She picked up the coin and put it in a round clay bank. She was saving up for her granddaughter's hope chest.

Faizeh paced back and forth for seven days and seven nights, raving and crying. She imagined going to the police and telling about how Amir killed

Munis. She also thought to kill him the way he had killed Munis. She thought of a thousand and one things, but none of them appealed to her. Finally she decided to bury the talisman at the foot of Munis's corpse on the night of the wedding, so that the blood of the corpse and the talisman would bring bad luck for Amir.

The night of the wedding, Faizeh went to Amir's house. She did so with Alia's cooperation, since Alia had a suspicion that Munis had been killed. So before leaving for Hajji's house, Alia let Faizeh in. Faizeh went straight to the garden and began to dig a hole for the talisman until a voice caused her to freeze. The voice belonged to Munis. It said, "Faizeh dear!"

It was as if she were calling out from the bottom of a well. Faizeh's mouth became dry. She put her hand on her chest as if she were trying to keep her heart from jumping right out of her body. The voice said, "Faizeh dear! I can't breathe!"

Faizeh remained silent. The voice said, "I'm very hungry. I'm dying of thirst. It's been ages since I had a little water or a seed to eat."

Faizeh began to dig with her fingers as if in a

trance. She dug and dug until Munis's round face appeared. She opened her eyes slowly and said, "Dear sister, give me a little water."

Faizeh went to the pool in the garden and brought some water in her hands and splashed it on Munis's face. Then she began to dig quickly. She dug and dug until she came out of the ground. She was so weak that she couldn't move. Faizeh picked her up and shook the dust off her body. When she staggered into the kitchen, Faizeh began to feel afraid. She did not know how to explain this strange incident. She cautiously tiptoed into the kitchen. She found Munis, covered with dust and dirt, stuffing fistfuls of food in her mouth with dirty hands. Her eyes rolled around in their sockets and she had a frightening smile on her face.

As she ate, she growled like a lion looking for her cubs. Finally, after finishing half a pot of food, she was sated. She got up and staggered out to the water pump in the yard and put a bucket under it, filled it up with dirty water, and gulped it down.

She stood still for a moment and then, making snorting noises, stripped naked, stepped into the pool in the garden, and began to wash herself.

Faizeh went up to her bedroom, which had not been touched. She took underwear, clothes, and a towel and returned to the yard. Munis took the towel and vigorously dried herself off. Then she got dressed, went into the living room, and sat down in her usual place by the radio. Faizeh, frightened, followed her into the living room and sat down in the corner across from her.

"Did you conspire with my brother to kill me? You shameless, disgraceful woman."

Faizeh shakily explained what had happened, but it was like talking to a stone.

"All your life you thought that my face was round and that because of that, I was an idiot, right?"

"What are you saying? Who could think such a thing?"

"You yourself, you bitch."

"I swear to God, I never thought such a thing."

Munis said, "You're an idiot. Now I can read minds. You not only thought that I was an idiot because my face is round, but also thought to take advantage of that stupidity and become my brother's wife, isn't that so?"

"I swear . . . "

"Shut up, don't swear to a lie."

Faizeh shut up. Munis said, "Now look, not only is my face not round, it's quite long."

Faizeh looked at her, and found to her astonishment that Munis's face was as long as a horse's face. Faizeh thought that she had a fever. She thought if only she were paralyzed, deaf, and blind, so that she wouldn't have to deal with these things. Munis said, "And besides that, the pupils of my eyes are long too."

Faizeh looked. She was right. The pupils of her eyes had become long. Munis said, "And not only are the pupils of my eyes long, but they're also red."

Faizeh saw that she was right. Her pupils were red and long. Faizeh thought that her feet must certainly be hooves, and then Munis said, "No, I don't have hooves."

She laughed demonically. Faizeh was about to pass out, but Munis wouldn't let her.

"Quit pretending. There's something dirty inside of you. But I've decided to live with you and leave this house. I want to found an organization to prevent other brothers from killing their sisters. But I'm really not a bad person. Just remember that I know whatever dirty thoughts you have in that little brain of yours. Get it?"

"Of course."

"My granny, may she rest in peace, had a cat that was trapped for twenty-four hours in a bundle of bedding. When it came out it was like a long, thin book. Then it ate so much that it swelled up and died. When I first came out from under the earth, I felt like that cat. I think that at that moment, the spirit of that poor cat entered my body."

"You are correct. Your eyes have become like a cat's. But your face has become like a horse's face."

"Why are you talking so formally? Until just a few weeks ago we were friends although you thought that I was an idiot. In any case we were friends. Talk like a normal person."

"Yes, ma'am."

"Besides, I read a book about men and women. From now on, don't think that you know more than me, get it?"

"Yes."

"By the way, I want you to know that Parvin is a better cook than you. That is my opinion. Understand?"

"Yes."

Faizeh's throat felt tight. Munis, who used to be a nice, simple girl with a round face, said, "Of course, your cooking isn't bad, but hers is better."

Then Faizeh asked, "Now what do we do?"

"We sit here like this until the bride and groom come."

A few hours later, the members of the household returned, accompanied by the parents of the bride and some of the guests. They called out shrilly, cheered, and shouted. With great fanfare they took the bride to the bridal chamber, and sent the groom, who was too drunk to walk straight, into the room after her. At that moment, Alia screamed and passed out, since she had seen Munis standing in the hallway, looking at the crowd.

Hajji Sorkhchehreh nodded toward Munis and asked, "Who might this lady be?"

Her mother, horrified, said, "Munis, my daughter."

Munis said nothing. The crowd divided to allow her through. She went to the bridal chamber. She pushed on the door, which, although it was locked from the inside, opened like the door of a dollhouse, and entered. Amir was taking off his clothes, and the girl, her face to the wall, was modestly undressing hers. At the sound of the door, they turned around, one in surprise, and one in shock. Munis lengthened her face and pupils and said, "Stop acting funny. Step forward like civilized people."

Amir came forward like a lamb.

"You poor slob, why are you so drunk?"

"What can I say?"

"You went and got an eighteen-year-old girl, chaste and obedient?"

"Yes."

Munis said to the girl, "And you, didn't you get pregnant by your cousin last year, and get an abortion from Madam Fatimi?"

The girl screamed and was about to pass out, but Munis prevented her from doing so, and said, "Stop pretending. You got my stupid brother drunk on the order of Madam Fatimi."

Then she turned to Amir and said, "And you, you bastard. You will have to get along with this woman. If you so much as raise your hand against her, I'll devour you in one bite. Understand?"

Amir nodded his head like a goat in a flock. The bride and groom were standing horrified before Munis. She said, "I'm going to live with Faizeh. That poor girl made a fuss but she really is a virgin. This one isn't, and that's what a stupid man gets. Anyway, as I said, if you harm her I'll punish you in a way that you'll never forget."

Munis left the room. Amir looked at his young bride, astonished and disappointed. Then he sat on the bed and burst into tears, saying, "What did I do to deserve this?"

He was wailing and crying, and the young bride again locked the door from the inside.

Munis walked toward the living room. Alia had come to, and fell in step behind her, along with Munis's mother and the rest of the crowd. Hajji Sorkhchehreh wanted to know why the groom's sister had not attended the wedding, but her mother could not interrogate her daughter in front of everybody. She also felt a vague fear of her.

Munis said to Faizeh, "Come on, let's go to Karaj."

Alia shouted, "For God's sake, take me with you."

Munis said, "Later, later."

The crowd watched quietly and in astonishment as the two women walked out the door and disappeared into the dark night.

Mrs. Farrokhlaqa Sadraldivan Golchehreh

Farrokhlaqa, age fifty-one, still beautiful and immaculately groomed, was sitting on a comfortable American rocking chair on the terrace. It was the middle of the spring, and the smell of orange blossoms filled the air. From time to time Farrokhlaqa closed her eyes and concentrated her entire being on the fragrance. She thought that if her father were still alive he would be sitting in the corner of the yard changing the soil in the geranium pots. Her father had died ten years ago, but it was as if he had just died yesterday. Two days before he died, he said, "Daughter, take care of yourself. I don't know about this man."

Farrokhlaqa forgot the fragrance of the flowers for a moment. The memory of her father was so strong that it overshadowed everything else. Involuntarily she covered her face with her hands. She wanted to escape the memory of the dead and the overwhelming sadness that it brought.

Golchehreh was in the living room. He was standing in front of the antique mirror, tying his tie. Part of the yard, the terrace, and Farrokhlaqa as she rocked gently back and forth were reflected in the mirror. Golchehreh extended the two-minute task to half an hour so that he could keep his wife under surveillance. He didn't want to look at her face to face. Every time he looked her in the face he could only smile with contempt. He couldn't help it. He didn't know why he felt such loathing whenever he looked at her. In fact, when he was far from her, or could watch her unobserved as he did now, he liked her. More than anything or anyone in the world. But whenever he had to face her, the old hatred welled up in him again. It was a thirty-year-old feeling.

Farrokhlaqa stretched, extending her arms wide and arching her back. She felt ecstatic. She recalled Vivien Leigh in *Gone with the Wind.* In one of the bedroom scenes she had stretched the same way. Whenever she thought of Vivien Leigh she thought of Fakhredin Azad. Her first memory of him was at the prince's party at Shemiran garden. Fakhredin had just returned from America. He had brought back slides and photographs of America to show everybody. The pictures of New York were so strange. Farrokhlaqa later went to New York three times, but she could never see the same New York that she had seen in those photographs. In her mind, it was all Golchehreh's fault. If she had gone to New York with Fakhredin, she would have seen that strange New York. But Golchehreh wasn't the one to show her that New York. All he did was eat breakfast in the hotel restaurant and spend the day sitting on a couch in the lobby until Entezami came and took them to a restaurant, a movie, or a show.

Golchehreh had finally finished tying his tie and was looking for a reason to remain standing in front of the mirror. It occurred to him that if he shaved, he could remain there for another half hour. He went to the bathroom, filled a bowl with warm water, and brought it with the shaving brush, the shaving cream, and a bib to the living room and began to shave.

Farrokhlaqa was patiently waiting for Golchehreh to finish what he was doing and go out. Since he retired, every evening he would go for a walk for a few hours, read a newspaper and get a cup of coffee in a cafe, and then return. And every day his wife waited patiently for him to go so that she could feel energetic and move about freely. Whenever he was in the house, she would lose her ability to move, and she would hide in a corner. She had a thirty-two-year-old habit of not moving. She had gotten used to immobility. She knew only this, and she knew it instinctively, that when Golchehreh went out, mobility and happiness would come to her. She used to be happier, since Golchehreh would be at work every day for at least eight hours, although he would come home for lunch and a nap. She had more energy to move back then. She even sang sometimes. With his retirement, she was deprived of this happiness. He was not only at home more often, but he was also annoying. It never occurred to him to fiddle with the flowerpots or adjust the grapevines or do something about the mosaics in the party room, which were falling off the walls. He was always wearing his pajamas, lying down on a sofa or on the floor to sleep, or teasing Farrokhlaqa with his pale and tasteless humor.

She said, "You should shave over the sink. You're getting the carpet wet."

Golchehreh's heart beat with joy as he swirled the shaving brush around in the water.

"Shut up!"

Farrokhlaqa bit her lip. She turned to face the yard. She didn't have the patience to answer him, although words were whirling explosively around in her head, trying to get out. But she held her breath. Fakhredin returned. He always came at times like this and saved her.

That night, the first night that she and Fakhredin met, he had come to her. Farrokhlaqa was standing under an acacia tree, and he came up behind her. She heard him say, "Vivien Leigh!"

Farrokhlaqa turned. Fakhredin was looking at her. She could still remember his mouth. Although she later kissed those lips many times, that first memory of them was unique. They mysteriously pressed together as if to conceal his perfectly white teeth.

"Who, me?"

"You, the delicate little sister of Vivien Leigh, such an amazing resemblance."

She wanted to look at him out of the corner of her

eye, over her left shoulder, a habit that she had inherited from her mother. She knew that she looked good when she did that. But before she could even turn her head toward her left shoulder, she lost her nerve. She was like a frightened bird. Fakhredin smiled.

"Farrokh, believe me, you become more and more beautiful every day. How is it possible?" She was nervous and alert.

At that point she was able to look at him out of the corner of her eye over her shoulder, and say, "It's been ten years."

"That I haven't seen you? How could that be?"

"Then where did you see me?"

Fakhredin patted his chest and said, "Here. Why did you get married?"

"I shouldn't have?"

"Did you have to?"

She was shocked. She had never promised him anything. When he went to America she was thirteen. She couldn't remember having any feeling for him. But at that moment, she thought that there could have been something.

"That's life. Everyone gets married."

"And you? How can such a beautiful woman get

married? You had absolutely no right to get married. You should have given the whole world the opportunity to see you."

Farrokhlaqa laughed softly. His manner of speaking was funny. He must have been annoyed by her laugh. But he wasn't annoyed, and came closer to her, and said, "You should always wear blue, it looks good on you."

At that moment Golchehreh showed up, more than a head shorter than Fakhredin, with that stale laugh and skeptical gaze that had been bothering her for four years, Fakhredin said, "I was just talking to your wife about *Gone with the Wind*. I saw it before I came back to Iran. It was one of the first nights that it showed. You can't imagine how much trouble it was to get a ticket. I got in line at five in the morning. I was telling your wife how much she looks like Vivien Leigh, the actress in the movie."

Golchehreh simply said, "How interesting!"

His smile, as always, was full of resentment. It was a smile of defeat. He was fair enough to realize that he somehow fell short of Fakhredin. Fakhredin said, "If it comes here, you should go see it. It's the greatest masterpiece of the cinema. And the most expensive movie ever made."

That night they went home in her uncle's car. Golchehreh sat silently the whole way home out of respect for her uncle. They said farewell politely at the entrance to the alley, and they walked slowly, side by side, toward the house. Farrokhlaqa was thinking the whole time that in an hour he would be asleep and she would have time to think before she went to sleep.

Golchehreh had not been in good form that night. In the alley he began to make nasty remarks about the "silly movies" about which that "pathetic guy" had spoken. About the stupid pictures. About that goofy hat that he had brought and put on everyone's head and taken pictures of them one by one. He had even taken a picture of Farrokhlaqa. Farrokhlaqa said with loathing, "Shut up!" The only advantage in saying this to Golchehreh was that it would make him shift his complaining to someone else. Now he left off of the "pathetic guy" and turned to her blue dress, saying how ugly and tacky it was, and how everyone had hated it.

He went down to the cellar and brought up a watermelon, and at two in the morning started to eat it, forcing her to eat it with him. She had been putting up with all this nonsense in the hope of having half an hour to let her thoughts wander before going to sleep. After eating the watermelon he decided to play with the radio, switching from the Berlin channel to the London channel to the Moscow channel to see what was going on in the world. Then at three o'clock in the morning he finally went to bed and of course before going to sleep he wanted to have sex. She put up with this, too, and then, at four o'clock, he decided to take a shower and pray, something that he did every now and then. From that night on, her heart was filled with loathing for him.

Golchehreh had finished shaving off his beard. Now he was slowly collecting his shaving things. He didn't know why he was procrastinating so much that day. It was as if he were waiting for something but didn't know what. The doorbell rang, and Mosayyeb went to the door. Farrokhlaqa waited patiently to find out who had come and what they wanted. Golchehreh came to the terrace and stood by his wife. Farrokhlaqa turned her head and looked at him for a moment. One look was enough for both of them to confirm their mutual hatred.

Golchehreh said abruptly, "Next month you'll be fifty-one years old. You have reached menopause, Farrokh dear."

Farrokhlaqa looked at him silently. His smile, as always, was derisive. Finally she said, "Listen, Sadri, if you think I'm going to put up with your jokes for even one second, I won't."

"I wasn't joking, dear. Menopause is not a laughing matter."

Farrokhlaqa took a deep breath. Mosayyeb returned with the newspaper and placed it at her feet. Then he said he was going to Karaj to buy meat from Nasrallah for Friday's party.

Farrokhlaqa said, "I wish we had a garden in Karaj."

"Do you think that after menopause you can still enjoy a garden?"

Farrokhlaqa, as she looked over the front page, said, "Are you wishing for a plump young woman to walk behind your coffin? Is that why you say such things?"

"Maybe I am. But my queen will not allow it."

"Fine, go find yourself a maid. You are really vile."

Absentmindedly she started to read the newspaper.

Golchehreh took it from her. She stared at the yard. Mosayyeb put on his coat and shoes and went to the door. As he passed by the garden pool, he asked, "Do you want anything else?"

"Get some fresh green almonds too if you can find them."

Mosayyeb left without saying anything. Golchehreh was sitting on the windowsill and fiddling with the newspaper. Farrokhlaqa thought, God, why doesn't he leave. She wanted to continue her fantasies.

She recalled the day when they had to go see Fakhredin's American wife. She had arrived six months after her husband with their two boys, Teddy and Jimmy. How strange those names had sounded. She would never forget how anxious she was that day. She curled her hair, and put on a white dress with blue flowers. Golchehreh laughed at her as she put on powder and lipstick and braided her hair. She spent a lot of time trying to get the seams of her pantyhose straight. At the last moment she spun around in front of the mirror. Everything seemed fine, but she hadn't seen the other woman yet. She had never seen an American woman before. But at least she had seen

Gone with the Wind with Vivien Leigh. She was not inferior to her, although she didn't see any resemblance. But if Fakhredin said there was a resemblance, there must have been one.

Fakhredin and his wife were staying at Sarim Mirza's house until their own house in the northern part of the garden was ready. The American woman was standing at the entrance of the five-door living room when they arrived, shaking hands with all the guests. She couldn't speak to anyone. She just smiled. She was an extremely tall woman, with blonde hair and hands covered with freckles and veins. Her eyes were so light that they seemed colorless. If you looked closely, you could see that they were blue, and Fakhredin was fond of the color blue. Farrokhlaqa shook hands with her and entered. There was a full-length mirror in the room, before which she stood and looked at herself. She stared for a while at her own dark eyes and the blue flowers on her dress. Fakhredin appeared behind her in the mirror, and asked, "Why did you get married?"

People had asked him the same question. But what a strange effect it had on her. The man was staring at her in the mirror, and Farrokhlaqa noticed that he was pale.

"This white dress with blue flowers looks really good on you."

He hurried over to his wife. That night, the whole night, he and Farrokhlaqa kept running into each other. It was as if a force was pulling them together.

Years later, on the moonlit terrace in the prince's garden, she told Adileh Rif'at all about that night. Adileh was a good woman. She had tried to understand. She thought that a woman had a right to love, and that love was worthwhile. She criticized Golchehreh's behavior. At that moment Farrokhlaqa's older daughter and Adileh's son were walking around the garden.

Rumors were circulating, and Farrokhlaqa knew that there was something between Adileh and Shazdeh. So she was telling her all about what happened to her, to loosen Adileh's tongue. It worked. Adileh cried and told everything. Farrokhlaqa said, "Eight years have passed, eight strange years."

"So throughout the war you were in love. Good for you."

Farrokhlaqa yawned and stretched. "Eight years of war."

Golchehreh was angry for no reason. Suddenly he asked, "When a woman reaches menopause, do her feelings change?"

"I don't know, Sadri."

"They must. That must be why every man has the right to marry several women, so that he doesn't always have to put up with a woman past menopause in his bed."

"Perhaps."

Golchehreh was thinking about a woman he had known, who had also been called Farrokhlaqa. She belonged to the war years. She was a Polish woman who didn't know Persian, and Golchehreh had called her Farrokhlaqa. She worked in a bar. Golchehreh used to call her Farrokhlaqa and she would laugh. She couldn't say the name properly, and it sounded funny to her. When the war was over, the woman said, "Farrokhlaqa go back Europe." Then she laughed. The next week, she wasn't in the bar anymore.

Golchehreh asked, "If I go and get another wife, you'll get angry!"

Farrokhlaqa didn't respond. She went back to looking at the garden. She recalled the last time she saw Fakhredin. They were in his house. They were in a room with the door closed and the curtains drawn. The room was dark, and his eyes shone in the darkness.

He said, "I have to go take care of my children."

Farrokhlaqa cried.

"I'll come back, I promise."

When the war was over, his American wife returned with Teddy and Jimmy. She was emotionally disturbed. One night at a party, she shouted, "You're all crazy!"

She was probably drunk, or perhaps she just couldn't take it anymore. Ten days later, she took her children and went home.

Farrokhlaqa didn't know why, but she knew that Fakhredin would not come back.

He didn't come back. Five months later he was killed in an automobile accident. Farrokhlaqa was left with her own problems and Golchehreh. There were children, but they were busy with their own lives. They grew up and left home so fast that it was as if they had never been born.

Golchehreh finished the newspaper and put it down, waiting for her to ask for it so that he could say something else about menopause. Actually, he had just come across this word for the first time three days ago, and he felt that it would somehow bother his wife. She said nothing, and Golchehreh got bored. Finally he asked, "You don't want the newspaper?"

The woman held her hand out without a word. Golchehreh gave her the paper. She took the paper and lit a cigarette.

Golchehreh said, "You shouldn't smoke. Especially at your age and in the middle of menopause."

"Why don't you go for a walk? You used to go every day."

"Maybe I don't feel like it today."

She regretted her question. If he knew that she was happy when he went out, he wouldn't go out anymore.

She said, "You're right, it's better for you to stay home."

"I'll go now."

He stood up. But for some reason, he felt that he had to stay. It seemed like something was about to happen. He walked over and stood before her in a daze. For a moment he thought that perhaps, after thirty-two years, he no longer needed to look at her with that smile. In fact, for some time he had known that he used this smile as a defense against her strange beauty. He knew that if he had not smiled that way, he would have been like a dead man to her by now. He knew that she must not, even for one moment, know how much he desired her. But now, all of a sudden, he had an urge. He wanted to look at her, just one time, the way he had looked at the Polish woman when he called her Farrokhlaqa. But now she had reached menopause. Her eyes were no longer rebellious. She no longer had any dreams at night. She went to bed early and even snored sometimes. Maybe he could look at her naturally now, without derision.

"Farrokhlaqa dear."

She trembled. He had never spoken to her that way. He always said Farrokh with that smile. She looked up. There was no derision in his eyes; he was looking at her kindly. Farrokhlaqa was frightened. She was certain that he was planning something. She thought, what if he kills me?

She punched him hard in the stomach. It was like a

pillow. He wasn't ready for the punch. He tripped over one leg and tried to regain his balance with the other, but lost control and fell down the terrace stairs. She stood in front of the chair for a while. She didn't dare look down the stairs. He didn't make a sound.

Three months later she was sitting on the chair wearing black. She was thin and weak. She did not like the house anymore. Mosayyeb brought a message from Mr. Ostovari, the realtor, saying that if she wanted to sell the house, she should not forget Ostovari. Farrokhlaqa, bravely and without reflection, told Mosayyeb to tell Ostovari to sell the house for her on the condition that he use the money to buy a garden in Karaj. Ostovari started looking for a garden.

He found a garden by a river.

Mrs. Farrokhlaqa Sadraldivan Golchehreh sold the house, bought the garden, and moved to Karaj.

Zarrinkolah

Zarrinkolah was twenty-six years old and a prostitute. She was working in the New City at Golden Akram's house. Akram had seven gold teeth and was also called Akram Seven. She had been there since she was a child. At first, she had three or four customers a day. By the time she was twenty-six, she had twenty to twenty-five or even thirty customers a day. She was tired of working. She had complained to Akram several times, and was yelled at and eventually beaten, until she shut up.

Zarrinkolah was a cheerful woman. She was always cheerful, whether she had three or four customers a day or thirty. She even turned her complaints into jokes. All the women liked her. When they ate lunch, Zarrinkolah would start joking and dance around the table, and the women would die laughing.

Several times she intended to leave the house, but

the women wouldn't let her go. They said that if she left the house it would be dead. Perhaps all the women encouraged Akram Seven to beat her. Zarrinkolah never really intended to leave, for if she left this house, she would have to go straight to another house. Once, when she was nineteen, she received a marriage proposal and had a chance to leave. The suitor was an ambitious construction worker who dreamed of becoming a mason, and who needed a hardworking wife. Unfortunately, before they could decide what to do, someone cracked open his skull with a shovel during a fight.

Although she complained sometimes, she had accepted her fate. But now, for six months, she had not been able to think clearly. The problem started one Sunday morning when she woke up.

Akram Seven shouted, "Zarri, there's a customer, and he's in a hurry."

There weren't many customers early in the morning. Usually just a few who had stayed over from the night before and had the urge in the morning. That Sunday morning, Zarrinkolah thought, so a customer has come. So what. She wanted to shout out, so what, but Akram Seven yelled, "Zarri, I'm talking to you. I said a customer has come."

She left her breakfast and angrily went back to the bedroom, lay down on the bed and opened her legs. The customer entered the room. It was a man without a head. Zarrinkolah didn't dare scream. The headless customer did his business and left.

From that day on, all of the customers were headless. Zarrinkolah didn't dare say a word about it. They might say that she was possessed by a demon. She had heard about a woman possessed by a demon, who would start shrieking at eight o'clock every night. For a while this scared away the customers until they kicked her out of the house.

Zarrinkolah decided to sing every night at eight o'clock so that she wouldn't shriek like that woman. She did this for six months. Unfortunately she couldn't carry a tune. A guitar player said, "You bitch, you don't even have a voice, you're giving everybody a headache." After hearing this, she went into the bathroom every night and sang there for half an hour. Akram Seven ignored it. After all, Zarrinkolah took care of thirty customers a day and was still cheerful. She was always cheerful.

Then they brought an innocent young girl to the house. One day Zarrinkolah took her into her room and said, "Kid, I have to tell you something. I have to tell somebody. I'm afraid I'm going crazy. I have a secret that's making me miserable."

The girl said, "Everyone has to tell their secrets to someone. My grandmother used to say that the poor Imam Ali, who couldn't talk to anybody, used to go out to the desert and put his head in a well and pour out his grievances."

"That's true. Now I'm going to tell you. I see everyone without a head. Not the women. The men. They're all headless."

The girl listened kindly. She asked, "You really see them all without heads?"

"Yes."

"OK, so maybe they really don't have heads."

"If they really didn't have heads, the other women would notice."

"Well, that's true. But maybe they all see them without heads, but like you, they don't dare say anything about it."

So they agreed that whenever Zarrinkolah saw a headless man she would let the girl know, and if the girl saw a headless man she would let Zarrinkolah know.

Zarrinkolah saw all the men without heads and the girl saw them all with heads.

The next day, the girl said, "Zarrinkolah, maybe you should pray and make a vow. Maybe then you'll see the men with heads."

Zarrinkolah took two days off work and went to the bathhouse. Instead of going to the public section like she usually did, she went to a private room so that she wouldn't have to talk and joke with the other women. She hired a bath worker to scrub her back. She washed herself from head to foot. She ordered the bath worker to scrub her three times. The bath worker scrubbed until Zarrinkolah's skin was raw. But she wasn't satisfied that she was clean enough to pray.

The bath worker finally broke down crying and said, "You poor woman, you must be crazy."

Zarrinkolah paid the bath worker well so that she wouldn't tell anybody about her, and asked her how to perform ablutions after sexual pollution.

When the bath worker left, Zarrinkolah performed ablutions. She did it fifty times. Her entire body was burning from the chafing of the sponge.

She intended to get dressed and go to the shrine of

Shah Abdulazim, but she had a sudden urge to pray. She decided to pray naked, but she didn't know how to pray. She decided that if Imam Ali was so sad that he went out to the desert to pour out his grievances to a well, it would be all right for her to just repeat his name as a prayer. She prostrated herself in prayer, naked in the bath, saying, "Ali Ali Ali Ali Ali Ali Ali Ali Ali Ali . . . "

As she was saying this she began to cry. She cried and called out to Ali.

Somebody knocked on the door, and then banged on it. She came out of her ecstasy and asked, sobbing, "Who is it?"

It was the bath attendant. She said they wanted to close up the bathhouse.

Zarrinkolah put on her clean clothes and gave her dirty clothes to the bath worker. She went out and walked to the shrine of Shah Abdulazim.

It was nighttime and the shrine was closed. She sat outside in the yard and cried quietly in the moonlight.

In the morning when they opened up the shrine, her eyes were swollen shut. She stopped crying, but did not enter. Her body felt like a piece of straw.

She ate breakfast in a diner. She asked the owner,

"If a person wants to drink cool water this time of the summer, where should she go?"

The owner looked at her puffy eyes with pity and said, "Karaj isn't bad."

There was nothing in her face to show that she had once been a prostitute. She had become a small woman of twenty-six with a heart as big as the sea.

She went to Karaj.

Two Girls on the Road

It was sunset. The two girls were on the road to Karaj. Each wore a chador. One was twenty-eight and the other was thirty-eight. They were both virgins.

Along the road a truck stopped near them. There were three men sitting in the truck. The driver and his assistant were drunk. The passenger was not drunk, and he had grabbed the steering wheel to avoid an accident several times as they drove, until he decided to sit still and put himself in the hands of fate.

The driver stopped the truck. The passenger stayed in the truck and lit a cigarette.

The driver and his assistant walked over to the two girls and the driver asked, "Where are you ladies headed?"

The twenty-eight-year-old, whose name was Faizeh, said, "We're going to Karaj to reap the benefits of our toil and get rid of the men who control us."

The driver laughed heartily and said, "Oh, really? Is that so?"

He pulled off her chador. She cried out for help. After a brief struggle, the women were overcome. Faizeh shouted out for help until the driver put his beefy hand over her mouth. The other one, whose name was Munis, silently endured everything that happened.

It didn't last more than fifteen minutes. The men stood up and, realizing that no one was coming to the rescue, calmly brushed the dirt off their clothes. The women were lying on the ground. Faizeh cried and said, "God damn them."

The men finished brushing themselves off. The assistant driver did not seem satisfied. He said, "Ismail, this one was like a rag doll."

"You get what you get. That one was a slut."

They both laughed. They thanked the women and went back to their truck. The passenger asked, "Did something happen?"

The driver said, "None of your business."

"Sorry, I thought maybe something had happened."

"Who do you think you are? Are you a cop?"

"No, I'm a gardener. They call me the good gardener."

The driver laughed and said, "Good gardener, we were watering the garden."

The driver and the assistant both laughed. They laughed so hard that the driver lost control of the truck. The truck spun around twice, barely missed a Mercedes coming from the opposite direction, and headed straight for the trees by the road. It knocked over the first tree, which was young, and smashed into the second, older tree and turned over. The door on the assistant's side of the truck opened, and before the truck had completely turned over, he fell under it. The driver crashed through the windshield and flew out into the sky. The passenger also crashed through the windshield, but he landed on a pile of hay and mud at a nearby construction site.

The driver grabbed a powerline as he flew through the air and started to do a little dance that actually wasn't too bad. The assistant driver didn't even have a chance to cry out, and he ended up with his entire body crushed under the truck. The passenger brushed the mud and hay off his clothes, saw the bodies of the drivers, and said, "What a crazy world!"

Finally he realized that in order to get the dirt off

himself he would have to take a shower and change his clothes.

He found the shoe that had come off his right foot, and he set off in the direction of Karaj.

Farrokhlaqa's Garden

Farrokhlaqa was sitting in the back seat of the car. Ostovari, Mosayyeb, and the driver were all in front. At four o'clock in the afternoon they arrived at the garden. Ostovari was a little bit tense. He was afraid that she would be angry when she saw the tree. He had told her all about the garden except for that one tree.

The driver stopped the car in front of the gate. Ostovari jumped out and opened the car door for her before the driver could do it. It was the driver's last day of work for her. Actually, he wasn't supposed to be working that day, but he had come along out of curiosity and to do her a favor. She knew how to drive.

Ostovari said, "Now you'll see what a jewel it is."

Farrokhlaqa went to the gate without a word, followed by Ostovari and Mosayyeb. She hesitated at the gate, turned her head over her left shoulder, a habit that she had inherited from her mother, and asked, "Is this it?"

Ostovari said, "Yes, ma'am."

He pulled a large key out of his pocket and said, "May I?"

He opened the door and stepped aside to allow her to enter. Farrokhlaqa gingerly stepped over the threshold. She shuddered with joy. She didn't want the men to notice. She calmly walked down the gravel path. Her eyes consumed the garden.

Ostovari came up alongside of her and said, "It's exactly what you wanted it. It just needs a few minor repairs."

She nodded. The gravel path led to the front of a house. In front of it was a large garden pool with a bench beside it. The path went around the garden pool and up to the steps of the house, which was covered with mosaics. It wasn't pretty. It had been built cheaply, and it showed. Farrokhlaqa was momentarily disappointed.

Ostovari said, "A layer of stucco would make it look like new."

Farrokhlaqa pictured it in her mind. It wasn't a bad idea. In any event, the windows were small, which suited the climate of the area.

Ostovari took out another key and opened the house. The door opened into a large, cool hall surrounded by three large rooms and a kitchen and a bathroom. The windows of the three rooms looked out on the garden, and the windows in the kitchen and bathroom looked out on the yard.

Farrokhlaqa said, "The kitchen is nice, but there's only one bathroom. And three rooms are not enough. I'll be having a lot of guests."

Ostovari said, "Ma'am, as I pointed out earlier, the foundation is sound and there are steel beams in the walls. You can add another floor. You can make the staircase to the second floor from here," he said, pointing to the corner of the room, "and if you want, you can plant a tree here that will grow up to the second floor and through the roof. It will be a palace."

The thought of having a tree in the house astonished her. Ostovari, bursting with pride, said, "That's my own idea."

Farrokhlaqa said, "But when you water the tree you might ruin the foundation."

Farrokhlaqa liked the house but didn't say so. She knew that she must not show any positive feelings in front of Ostovari. But her fantasies had begun. She was sure that she would add a second floor. She was planning a busy social life, and already had visions of all her friends in Tehran coming to visit. She didn't have many friends. Thirty-two years with a bad-tempered, solitary man had cut her off from many of them. But she still had time to find friends. Real friends, literary types. She could turn her house into a literary salon, just like the French ladies in novels.

Ostovari showed her the garden. She would have to hire a gardener to take care of the garden. It was obvious that it had been left untended for a year. He led her from tree to tree, telling her about each one.

He said, "Ma'am, if you searched all of Karaj you couldn't find a nicer garden. I mean it. There are nice houses and nice gardens here, but for this price this is the best. With a little touching up, it will be a paradise."

Farrokhlaqa knew that he was just being a salesman, but she didn't care. She had liked the house and garden from the first moment. There was no need for his sales pitch.

They finally arrived at the riverbank.

Ostovari said, "As you can see, this side doesn't have a wall. The river is the boundary. It runs so fast here that there is no danger of intruders. Besides, there aren't any burglars around here."

"I see."

And she saw the tree. She wasn't sure if it was real. She asked, "Who's that?"

Ostovari thought, here we go. He said, "This . . . well, actually, it's a person. But it's the most harmless person that you've ever seen in your life."

"Well, what's it doing here?"

Ostovari said, "How can I put this. In fact, this is why they are selling the garden for such a low price. I didn't want you to miss the opportunity. It's impossible to find a garden at such a price. I thought it would be all right, especially since you're a woman. Surely you won't mind this poor tree."

Farrokhlaqa stepped forward hesitantly. "But this isn't a tree, it's a person."

"True. The fact is that this poor tree . . . is actually the sister of the garden's former owner."

"How strange!"

"Yes, it is. The poor woman lost her mind and planted herself in the earth."

"That's impossible. If she's insane, they should put her in a mental hospital."

"Well, that's the problem. The poor woman disappeared last fall. Her family looked all over the city and the countryside for her, but couldn't find her. Finally, at the beginning of the summer, they came to the garden to get a breath of fresh air, and discovered that the poor thing had planted herself in the ground. So now they think she's crazy. But ma'am, no matter how hard they try, they can't get her out of the ground."

Ostovari pulled out a large handkerchief and wiped away a few tears. Farrokhlaqa was touched.

"Mr. Ostovari, is she a member of your family, God forbid?"

"No, ma'am. I swear to God, it's been at least twenty years since I cried. I don't know why, but every time I see the poor thing I begin to cry. . . . Anyway, no matter how hard they try, they can't get her out of the ground. She begs them, 'For God's sake, don't cut me, let me grow green.'"

"But she hasn't grown leaves."

"No, she hasn't, but she's sprouted roots. Maybe next year she'll grow leaves."

"So what about her family?"

"What can I say? They are completely beside themselves with the disgrace. What are they supposed to say? My daughter, my sister has become a tree? You can't say that to people. Anyway, they came to consult me. They said they would sell the garden cheap on the condition that their name be withheld. I promised to do so. That's why it's so cheap. In any case, it's your luck."

"So why are they ashamed of her? Becoming a tree is nothing shameful."

"Ma'am, how can it not be shameful? You think a normal person turns into a tree? Only someone like this poor, crazy woman could turn into a tree. Her brother cried in front of me and said, 'Any minute now people are going to find out that my sister has become a tree, and start gossiping about us. They'll say, it's the Treemans or the Treesons, and then they'll always be writing things on our house, and a century of our family's reputation will be ruined.' Ma'am, I can tell you that they are a respectable family. How can they say that one of their relatives is a tree? If she had become a government official or a representative that would be something to brag about. But what do you say about becoming a tree? Her poor brother used to say, even if she became a yoghurt maker, that would be something, we wouldn't mind. Yoghurt making, that's work. But a tree, I really don't know."

Farrokhlaqa was walking around the tree. Mosayyeb and the driver were looking on from afar. They didn't dare approach.

The tree was a woman of twenty-seven or twenty-eight. She was buried knee-deep in the ground and clad in rags. She was standing stiffly and looking at Farrokhlaqa and Ostovari. Farrokhlaqa felt that she was beginning to like the tree.

Ostovari said, "I said to her brother, 'Don't worry, sir. I know a respectable woman from a good family, a real lady. She will certainly be able to put up with poor Mahdokht in her garden. And she'll keep your secret. She's respectable, so she knows what it means to have a reputation."

Farrokhlaqa wasn't listening. Suddenly a brilliant idea occurred to her. She was thinking of all the things that she could do with this strange tree. She could not only establish a literary salon, but could also become a government official or a representative. She had never heard of anyone who had a human tree.

Ostovari said, "As I said, you could plant another tree inside the house to make up for this one. You could build a wall around this one to conceal it so that it doesn't cause a disgrace."

Farrokhlaqa thought, when you have a human tree, you don't need a tree in the house. She always knew that her mind, spirit, and body were superior. Other people really didn't deserve to understand the meaning of a human tree. Farrokhlaqa herself didn't exactly understand the problem, but her instincts told her that this tree would bring her fame.

"Mr. Ostovari, there's no need for a tree in the house. And this tree will remain as is. I accept it the way it is."

Ostovari breathed a sigh of relief, and said, "I was thinking all along that you wouldn't accept it. I thought that if you didn't want the garden, I would buy it. But, ma'am, I have six children. I am sure that the children would pull this poor tree up by the roots."

Farrokhlaqa headed for the garden gate. She wasn't listening to Ostovari anymore. As she walked, she called out, "Mosayyeb, Akbar, go to the city and bring everything here."

Mosayyeb asked, "Are you staying here tonight? The house is empty."

Farrokhlaqa said, "It doesn't matter. I'll stay here beginning tonight. I want to supervise the work. Mr. Ostovari, would it be possible to bring a few workers here? I want to start the renovations tomorrow."

Ostovari asked, astonished, "Ma'm, what's the rush? You can stay in the city for now. I can supervise the work. Mosayyeb can help."

"No. I'll stay myself. I want to get it done in a month."

Someone was knocking at the gate. Mosayyeb passed in front of her as she went to open it, and said, "You shouldn't stay here now. The villagers don't know you, and they're nosy. See? They're already knocking at the gate."

"It's okay, I'll teach them not to bother me."

Mosayyeb opened the gate. It was a man and a woman. The man said, "Excuse me, young man, does this house need a gardener?"

Farrokhlaqa came up behind Mosayyeb. Before he could answer, she said, "Why? Are you a gardener?"

The man said, "Yes, ma'am, I am. They call me the good gardener. They say I have a green thumb. If I touch a branch, it becomes a hundred branches with a hundred flowers on every branch."

Farrokhlaqa felt that her soul was changing. She had a human tree, and now a man with a kind face who claimed that he had a green thumb.

She asked, "Do you know how to do construction work too?"

"I know all kinds of work, ma'am. All kinds."

"Who's this? Your wife?"

The gardener looked at the woman who was standing beside him and said, "No, ma'm. I found this poor woman on the road to Karaj. She was standing there looking confused. When she saw me she screamed, fell at my feet, and began to cry. So I asked her, why are you crying? She kept kissing my feet. Finally she said that I was the first man she had seen in six months who had a head."

Farrokhlaqa asked, "Is she crazy?"

"I don't think so. When I started on my way she

followed me. She says her name is Zarrinkolah. She says that once she did bad things but that she has repented."

Farrokhlaqa asked the woman, "Zarrinkolah, can you cook?"

"No, ma'am."

"Can you sweep?"

"No, ma'am."

"How about dishes?"

"I don't know, ma'am."

"Then what can you do?"

"I can learn all these things, ma'am. But I know stories, and lots of songs. I know other things too. I'm young, but very experienced, ma'am."

Farrokhlaqa turned to the gardener and asked, "What's your name?"

"What's the use of knowing my name? Everybody calls me the gardener. You can call me gardener."

"I'll hire you. But what should we do with that woman?"

"Take her on, ma'am. She can do odd jobs. She'll learn."

"All right."

She thought she could make a good servant out of her. She didn't look bad, though she seemed a little naive.

Then she turned to Mosayyeb and the driver and said, "Go and bring as much as you can from the house. The suitcases and carpets are packed. You might have to use a truck, which is fine. I want everything here tonight. Mr. Ostovari, take the gardener with you to town and buy construction tools and supplies."

"Ma'am, it's six o'clock. Everything is closed."

"Enough talk, Mr. Ostovari. After all, we have a secret. We must help each other."

"Certainly."

Farrokhlaqa said to the woman, "You stay with me."

"Yes, ma'am."

As soon as the men left, someone knocked on the door. Farrokhlaqa opened it. It was two tired-looking women in dusty chadors.

Farrokhlaqa asked, "What do you want?"

One of the women started to cry. The other one, who was older, waited silently for her companion to finish crying.

"I said, what do you want?"

The woman who had been silent answered, "Ma'am, how do you do. My name is Munis. This is my friend Faizeh. We've come a long way, and we're extremely tired. Bad things have happened to us. If you would permit us, we would like to spend the night in your house. Tomorrow we'll see what fate has in store for us."

"Ladies, I've just arrived. I have no furniture. It's very strange for two ladies like you to be out here in the middle of nowhere. From your appearance it is clear that you are from respectable families. Why are you traveling alone?"

Munis said, "It's a long story. The problem is, we decided to escape from the prison of family life. We travel around and go on pilgrimages. Unfortunately, the first place we chose was Karaj, where this disaster happened."

Farrokhlaqa was interested. "Please come in. My furniture will be arriving tonight. Do come in and tell me what happened to you."

The women entered and sat on the bench by the garden pool. Faizeh was crying softly.

Farrokhlaqa said, "She shouldn't cry so much. It's not good for her health."

Zarrinkolah said, "Actually, it's very good for her health, ma'am. I cried for twelve hours yesterday. My eyes are not usually like this. They are really very big. But crying made me feel better. Let her cry."

Farrokhlaqa said, "Faizeh, what happened? Say something."

Faizeh kept crying.

Munis said, "Let me tell you, ma'am, I was thinking of going to India and China to see the world. I want to comprehend everything, and not just sit around and let other people tell me what's what and make an ass of me for the rest of my life. They say that ignorance is bliss. But I've decided to take a risk and seek knowledge. Of course it's dangerous to walk along the road. Either you're strong enough to face the danger, or you're not, and you return like a lamb to the flock. Maybe when you go back, they'll act like you have the mange and shun you. There are only two possibilities: either you endure the shunning or you don't, and you kill yourself.

"In any event, it worked out that this old friend of mine became my traveling companion, since I was afraid to leave her alone. I was afraid she would do something terrible to herself, or to someone even less fortunate than her. I really don't know why I thought that if I wanted to get out of Tehran, I had to go to Karaj. Now that I think about it, Tehran is close to Mehrabad, Ray, and Niyavaran. In fact, it's close to a thousand places. But I thought only of Karaj. So we set out on the road, and a truck stopped. The drivers got out and raped us. Of course I see a deeper meaning in all this. I think that some power wanted me to face an obstacle at the beginning. But poor Faizeh was sacrificed for my sake. She's been crying ever since. I think that with this rape, I have taken the first step toward discovering some logical order. This is the first bitter experience of traveling. On the way I thought about how millions of people drowned so that the first person could learn to swim. The amazing thing is that people still drown. Never mind, saying these things doesn't make Faizeh feel any better."

Faizeh, sobbing, said, "Ma'am, I was a virgin. I was a virgin. I want to get married some day. What will I do now that this disgrace has ruined my reputation?"

Munis said, "Well, Faizeh dear, I was a virgin too. To hell with it. We were virgins, now we're not. It's nothing to cry over."

"Honey, you're thirty-eight, what good does virginity do you? I'm twenty-eight. I still have a chance to get a husband."

Farrokhlaqa was thinking what a rude woman she was, to say something like that about her friend's age.

Munis said, "No, Farrokhlaqa, she's not rude. The poor thing knows that I read minds. When she thinks about something, I know what she's thinking. So she's learned to be frank with me."

Faizeh said, "You can transform your face and eyes. Why didn't you take revenge for us?"

"Faizeh dear, I only read minds. I wanted to take revenge, but they ended up paying for it anyway."

"How?"

"Two kilometers from where it happened, their truck crashed. So why was I supposed to take revenge?"

"That's a lie. What do you mean, their truck crashed?"

"Sweetie, we took a shortcut through the mountains so that we wouldn't get raped again. But I know that the truck crashed."

"How do you know?"

"I just know. I read minds."

Farrokhlaqa said, "Do you really read minds?"

"Yes, ma'am. For example, you want to become a representative. That poor thing over there was a prostitute until yesterday. Just like that. Nothing is hidden from me."

Farrokhlaqa said, "Would you like to stay here?

"Of course. Unfortunately, this is not a good time for a woman to travel alone. She has to be invisible to travel, or just stay at home. I can't stay home any longer, but because I am a woman, I must stay home somewhere. I can make a little progress, then get stuck in a house, then go a little further, and get stuck in another house. At this rate I might be able to go around the world at a snail's pace. That's why I accept your invitation with pleasure."

Farrokhlaqa was extremely happy, and said, "Ladies, I want to expand this house. The gardener told me that he also knows how to do construction work. He's the only man that we keep here. We're going to manage the construction work ourselves."

Munis said, "That's a very good idea. I knew all this before. God willing, everything will work out."

Faizeh was still crying.

Farrokhlaqa said, "What's wrong now? Can't you live without your virginity? I've been living without it for thirty-two years."

Faizeh said, "But ma'am, what about my reputation? How do I explain that to my family or my husband? What will I do on my wedding night?"

Munis said, "If you ever get married, I will make it so that your husband won't know. Don't worry. You know that I can transform my face."

"So why didn't you do it in front of those monstrous drivers?"

"Faizeh dear, I died and was reborn twice. Now I see things differently. How can I explain it to you? I swear to God, if I had wings, I would fly. The unfortunate thing is that even though I died twice, my soul is still of this world. By God, believe me, virginity is not important. I swear to God, I will arrange things so that if you find a husband, you will be accepted into his house."

Faizeh finally quieted down, and while the women waited for the furniture and baggage and construction supplies to arrive, they told each other about their lives.

The Garden

In the spring, the garden was a garden. The gardener was right. He had a green thumb. All he had to do was touch a branch and a week later it would have a thousand buds.

They had done the repairs on the house. Farrokhlaqa didn't work. She spent the entire fall walking around and giving orders. The gardener taught the women how to do construction work. Zarrinkolah made mud plaster, Munis carried the plaster into the building, Faizeh hauled bricks and the gardener oversaw the construction. The house had six rooms and three bathrooms by the end of the fall.

Farrokhlaqa would sit by the pool on sunny days and happily observe the work. Sometimes she took Zarrinkolah with her to town to shop. The house was being built according to Farrokhlaqa's taste. She would give an order and the gardener would take care of it.

At the end of the fall the house was finished. Farrokhlaqa gave Munis and Faizeh a room. The women were her companions, and also did the housework. Faizeh cooked and Munis did the rest. Farrokhlaqa decorated the house and gave the gardener permission to build a little house for himself at the end of the garden. He told Farrokhlaqa that he could do this with Zarrinkolah's help.

The gardener built his little house on the river bank, facing the tree of Mahdokht, which was still without fruit. Farrokhlaqa worried about it, but the gardener assured her that by spring it would be covered with blossoms.

He said, "You can't treat it like the other trees. It's a human tree. It must be fed with human milk."

Farrokhlaqa didn't know where to get human milk.

The gardener said, "Don't worry. I want to marry Zarrinkolah. She'll have my baby. Then she'll have milk that I can use to feed the tree."

Faizeh suggested that they bring in a mullah and have a ceremony. The gardener didn't want to. He explained that he would read the rites himself and didn't need a mullah. Faizeh wouldn't accept this as a marriage.

Munis was silent. She didn't say anything about what she knew from reading minds.

Farrokhlaqa concluded that it didn't matter. She wanted human milk for the tree and the gardener would get it from Zarrinkolah. That was that.

Zarrinkolah was always with the gardener. She worked with him. The gardener taught her construction work, gardening, cooking, and embroidering. She sang and wandered around all day. She was always everywhere and nowhere, and this made Faizeh resent her. Faizeh thought that she was a cheap and careless woman who was always laughing to get attention. Faizeh couldn't stand people like that. Of course she was happy with her life, but every time she remembered Amir she felt a pang of sadness. She wasn't averse to the idea of somehow becoming his wife. She didn't love him anymore. Nor did she want a husband. It would just be a victory for her. She wanted to become his wife in order to win.

Farrokhlaqa was seriously thinking about becoming a representative. She waited impatiently for the work to get finished so that she could invite important men to the house. After talking it over with Munis, she concluded that she had to start her social life by becoming famous. Munis suggested that she write poetry and publish it in newspapers and magazines. Farrokhlaqa approved of Munis's idea, and thought day and night about composing poetry.

By the beginning of the winter the house was completely ready and the women had settled in. Farrokhlaqa prepared a party room with cushions and chandeliers. She ordered fifty volumes of poetry and arranged the books in the party room. She bought large candleholders in the shape of butterflies to impress the guests. She ordered that the cellar be filled with wine and vodka so that there would always be plenty to drink.

Then she invited the guests. They came every Friday and stayed from morning until late at night. Farrokhlaqa slaughtered a sheep every Friday. The butcher would skin it and chop it into pieces, and Munis and Faizeh would cook it. Zarrinkolah would flutter around the women doing trivial things. The house became famous. Farrokhlaqa never said anything about the tree that was Mahdokht. At the gardener's suggestion, she was waiting for it to grow leaves before telling anybody about it.

In February Zarrinkolah no longer came to the

main house. She spent all her time at the gardener's house. Farrokhlaqa asked the gardener about it. He said that Zarrinkolah went out with him every morning at dawn to look for dew with which to irrigate the tree. She still wasn't pregnant, so she still didn't have any milk.

Munis, who could not read the mind of the gardener, asked to share in this work with them. The gardener agreed. Throughout February and March the three of them collected dew from the plants and trees in the garden, and the gardener used it to water the tree in a secret way.

The tree blossomed in the middle of March. It sang songs with the birds, filling the garden with music. Farrokhlaqa wanted to show the tree to the guests, but the gardener refused.

He said, "It's not time yet."

Even Farrokhlaqa was not allowed to see the tree. Because of this she sometimes felt a touch of resentment. She made an effort to suppress this feeling. She needed the gardener so much that she had to do everything he said.

She was also busy composing poetry. Every Friday, journalists, poets, painters, writers, and photographers would come to her house, and Farrokhlaqa still had no poetry to read in order to become famous. Munis commiserated with Farrokhlaqa whenever she had spare time.

Faizeh was pessimistic about the way things were going. Of course, out of fear of Munis, she didn't dare think about it. But whenever Munis was far enough away that she couldn't read her thoughts, Faizeh would mull over these problems and conclude that everything that was happening was stupid. Faizeh thought that this whim to write poetry was round-faced Munis's fault, who in spite of all of the things that she could do, including making her face long, was round-faced, stupid and simple-minded by nature.

April arrived and Farrokhlaqa still hadn't composed any poetry.

Suddenly, one day at ten in the morning, a flood of people invaded the garden. Of course they came every week, but not in such numbers. Farrokhlaqa anxiously put Munis and Faizeh to work, and looked around for Zarrinkolah. She was extremely angry that the lazy woman was sitting around eating when there were a hundred guests in the garden. She yelled at the gardener like a madwoman, and he appeared out of nowhere in the midst of the uproar.

"Tell that wife of yours to give these women a hand. They're swamped with work."

"I can't, ma'am. She became pregnant yesterday and mustn't lift a finger for nine months."

Now Farrokhlaqa was really mad and said, "In the first place, how do you know that your wife became pregnant last night? And what am I supposed to do with all these guests?"

"Don't worry. We'll make the tree sing. The guests will all become calm. They'll forget their hunger, and the food will remain for you. From now on, don't invite anyone until you've composed poetry. What's the point of them coming and eating all your food when they don't help with anything?"

The gardener went away, and the tree started to sing. All over the garden, the guests fell silent. It was as if there was a drop of water seeping down into the ground, and all of the people were within this one drop, which was like an ocean containing them all. The drop that was like an ocean went down to the depths of the earth, where it mingled with the sensation of the soil, millions of particles were the guests in the water and the soil, in a dance that began and would never end. A dance so fast that the synchrony of the hands and feet became mixed up. The dancing essence was absorbed by the roots and began to move through the rhythm and melody of the wood. The pith of the tree was like a bunch of ropes hanging from the ceiling of the sky. Munis whispered in Farrokhlaqa's ear, "Look how the sky surrounds us. This is another sky, a sky in a sky in a sky in a sky . . . "

Farrokhlaqa saw that she had closed her eyes and was staring at the sky from behind her eyelids. She crossed her legs and watched with a peculiar sense of pleasure as the guests, astonished, tried to follow the infinite extension of the pith. . . . Then a green illusion began. A greenish fog enveloped everyone. The earth and the sky were green. Green permeated all the colors of the spectrum. The people scattered in the fog, in which they were absorbed, and were finally dropped from the ends of leaves in the form of dew. This went on until evening. Then the tree fell silent and the guests, speechless and intoxicated by the tree's singing, left the house.

Farrokhlaqa didn't invite anyone after that. She promised herself that she wouldn't invite anyone until she composed poetry. Every day she shut herself into the party room and tried to do so.

Munis spent most of her time with the gardener in his wife. Zarrinkolah had stopped talking ever since she became pregnant. She sat silently by the window and looked out at the river. Munis and the gardener collected the dew every morning at dawn, and while they fed the tree they fed Zarrinkolah as well. She was changing slowly. As she grew fatter, she changed color. She was becoming transparent. Little by little it became possible to see right through her.

Munis would sometimes stand behind Zarrinkolah and look through her body at the river. She was always sitting facing the river, watching the water flow by.

At the other end of the garden Faizeh was left alone. No more guests came to eat her cooking and compliment her on it. Munis was never around, the gardener's wife had disappeared, and it was no longer possible to talk to the gardener. He was always busy. Faizeh got tired of being alone. Sometimes she went to Tehran just to walk around. She planned her walks so that she would pass by Amir's house. When she ran into him, they would nod to each other.

By the end of the summer Farrokhlaqa had made some progress with meter and rhyme. It was August, and after three months, she finally emerged from the room and went to sit by the pool. Munis was watering one of the flower beds. Farrokhlaqa asked her to come over so that she could read her a poem.

She said, "Of course, Munis dear, it's not really a poem. But I think that if I keep working at it I will be able to compose a real poem after a few years."

Munis insisted that she read her poem.

"I must say, it's not really a poem. It's just an attempt to come up with some meter and rhyme." Munis again insisted.

Farrokhlaqa blushed with excitement and recited:

O sugar bowl without sugar, O anvil without a
  shoemaker
O laughter without a laugh, O yard without a
  raker
O houri, O just one, O snake-hearted creature in
  the sand
O coquette, O fairy, O sad one without a saltshaker

O you without wings and feathers with a broken leg
O soothing one come and be a dreammaker
You traveled, you left, you packed, you did not see
O mirror of the heart, me sitting here nibbling on a cracker
What must one want from this crazy world of need
What must one say to this soulless monkey without a tracker
I am depressed, sorrow does not help my war
Kill my heart, be a giver and taker
Fari is depressed, such a small, ruined temple
She craves her beloved, won't he dance, the heartbreaker

Farrokhlaqa fell silent. Munis looked at her feet, not saying anything. Farrokhlaqa watched her anxiously.

Finally she said, "What do you think? Of course I know it's full of mistakes. But I've never composed a poem before. This is my first attempt."

"Give it to me and I'll read it. I didn't understand it right when you read it to me."

Farrokhlaqa gave it to her. Munis began to read it carefully. Farrokhlaqa's heart was pounding. Of course she knew that Munis was not knowledgeable about poetry, but in any event she was a person who could read minds. She had some good qualities that could not be ignored. Farrokhlaqa nervously glanced around at the tree and the water in the pool.

Finally Munis spoke. "Why did you put the sugar bowl without sugar at the beginning?"

Farrokhlaqa was expecting exactly this question. She smiled and said, "You see, I pay a lot of attention to objects, and have often looked at sugar bowls. A sugar bowl without sugar seems very sad."

Munis nodded and said, "Certainly, it must. But this anvil without a shoemaker is a bit strange. An anvil seems like it ought to belong to a smith, not a shoemaker."

Farrokhlaqa was surprised. She wanted to say no, it belongs to a shoemaker, but she wasn't certain. She asked, "Are you sure?"

"I don't know. As far as I know, it belongs to a smith."

"So what do you call the thing that a shoemaker has?"

Munis thought for a minute. Although she had a good memory, she couldn't recall. She said, "God, I don't know."

"This is bad. If I change the shoemaker to a smith now, I'll mess up the rhyme."

"It might not be bad to change it to a smith. As it is, some of the rhyme words don't make sense. Like a sad one without a saltshaker, or nibbling on a cracker, or be a giver and a taker, none of which fits correctly. You could use new rhyme words to go with smith. Then again, there's this snake-hearted creature in the sand. Of course, people may like that, but I don't understand what it means. Or this about a dancing heartbreaker."

Farrokhlaqa's morale was broken. Munis knew that her dreams were shattered.

"Don't fret over poetry. There are other ways to succeed. I read the mind of this painter who was here last time, and he wants to paint a picture of you. Let him do it. Give him good money and he'll definitely do it. That way you'll hook up with famous people. Anyway, you're already well-connected. Approach people sincerely, and tell them that you want to be elected to congress. They'll help you out."

Farrokhlaqa stopped dwelling on her shattered dreams and considered Munis's suggestion.

She said, "I think I have to start having parties

again beginning next week. I must tell Mosayyeb and Akbar to come back. We need servants here to do the work for the party."

And that is what happened. Beginning the following week the guests came. Family and friends began to frequent the garden. Amir came a few times with the excuse of seeing his sister. He no longer dared to boss her around. He came politely without his wife.

Faizeh asked him, "Amir, why didn't you bring your wife?"

"She's busy, ma'am. Besides, she's not sharp enough for this kind of thing. She's a housewife."

"I really don't like housewives at all. A wife ought to be social. A wife ought to help her husband get ahead in society. She shouldn't just sit in the kitchen. Take you, for example—how long do you want to remain an office worker? Eventually you have to move up. The way to do that is to associate with important people. Now I know more important people here than I can count. I can get anything done if I say the word."

Amir asked, "Do you know Mr. Aterchiyan too? He's the one who was here last week. He's short, red-faced, and bald."

"Of course, you're talking about Mr. Monaqabi's opium-smoking companion. He's always here."

Amir's eyes lit up. Every time he saw Faizeh, he would mention Aterchiyan's name. She would ask Amir what business he had with him, but was too clever to offer her services for free.

Farrokhlaqa became the painter's model. The painter came every Tuesday and Friday to paint her portrait. It was decided that they would have an exhibit of portraits of Farrokhlaqa from different angles. He had gotten so much money from her that he was willing to have ten exhibits of portraits of her.

Munis usually stayed at end of the garden, helping the gardener collect the dew. Mosayyeb and Akbar did the cooking. The women no longer had to work.

At the beginning of the winter, Farrokhlaqa thought about getting rid of the women. Now she knew how to handle things. The exhibit opened in November. She thought about setting up a household in Tehran so that she could spend the summer in the garden and the winter in the city. The women were really getting on her nerves.

One night in the middle of the winter the garden was filled with light. Munis was sleeping by the window. She opened her eyes and saw the light and said, "She's giving birth."

She got dressed and went to the end of the garden. The garden was covered with snow and bathed in light, as if it were the beginning of the world.

Zarrinkolah, who had become crystal clear, was one with the light.

The gardener was sitting against the wall and patching his cloth shoes.

Munis said, "We must help her."

"She's giving birth by herself. A real woman gives birth by herself."

At dawn a lily was born. The gardener took the lily to the river. Earlier he had dug a small hole there. The water in the hole had frozen. The gardener carefully placed the lily on the ice.

Munis said, "It'll die this way."

"It won't die. It'll sprout roots."

They went back to the room. The woman was sitting silently on the bed. She was no longer crystal clear. She had become herself again with breasts full of milk. The gardener hugged her and stroked her hair. He kissed her hands and rubbed her feet.

He said, "Now we must give milk to the tree."

He gave her a container, and she filled it with her milk.

The gardener said, "Now go to sleep, and sleep well."

He picked up the container, and he and Munis went to the tree. He said, "It's frozen. That's good—it's hibernating. By spring it will be unlike any tree you've ever seen."

The gardener dripped the milk into the ground at the foot of the tree until sunrise. Then he returned to his house.

Munis walked back to the main house through the bare trees. She had died twice, and nothing surprised her anymore. Along the way she leaned against a tree and said, "I need help."

She was jealous of the prostitute. The prostitute had won easily. Turning into light had been as easy for her as laughing. Munis didn't know the secret. She asked, "What should I do to become light?"

There was no answer.

She didn't feel like she could become a tree; that wasn't in her nature. Nor was she one to give birth. She knew that she was rotten inside. She was rotten from waiting. She knew that it was love that led to the feeling of light. She had never experienced love. She had been confused, but love, that was a distant ocean. Both far and near. She knew that if she could touch the rough bark of a tree with the tips of her fingers, really touch it, love would come. But she always sensed the roughness of the bark before she touched it. She always knew the roughness of the tree, the baseness of man. She herself was not base, but she knew baseness. She hadn't learned it, she knew it.

There, in the wilderness of Karaj, she had known unbridled passion. Unfortunately, before experiencing it, she had known passion already. The problem was that she knew everything on an intellectual level, so that she had repressed real experience out of fear of disgrace. She wanted to be an ordinary person, without really knowing the secret of being ordinary. She had never understood the meaning of poverty, and thus had never and would never have any wealth. She had never liked earthworms, felt humble before a dry leaf, prayed with the song of the swallow, climbed a mountain, watched a sunrise, stared at the big dipper from sunset to dawn. She had seen the dirt and sand as if they were the same, but she distinguished between the sky and the earth, so she never saw the sky in the earth nor the earth in the sky. She saw that she had a tendency to rot, and that she was rotting. She thought, so what can I do? What can I do with my trivial knowledge? How can I get past it?

Farrokhlaqa woke up and stood in front of the house in a wool robe. When she saw Munis she said, "The house is freezing, did you leave the door open?"

Munis said, "I'm sorry."

She knew that Farrokhlaqa wanted them to leave. She said, "What do you think I can do with my trivial knowledge?"

"What trivial knowledge?"

"This trivial knowledge. For example, you want us to leave. Why must I know this?"

Farrokhlaqa shrugged her shoulders. She had learned how to deal with Munis. She no longer feared her ability to read minds. She knew that it was not important. She was too simple a woman to make use of this knowledge. It just made her life difficult.

Farrokhlaqa said, "Today I'm going to the city. I've rented a house. You can stay as long as you want. I'll be back next summer. Give the keys to the gardener so that he can give them to me."

Mahdokht

Mahdokht planted herself on the riverbank in the fall. She groaned throughout the fall. Her feet were slowly frozen into the ground. The cold autumn rains tore her clothes to shreds. She was left half naked in rags. She shivered until winter came, and then she froze. Her eyes remained open the entire time, looking at the running water. The first spring rains broke up the ice on her body. She realized that tiny new leaves were growing out of her fingers. Her toes rooted her feet to the ground. In the spring she listened to the sound of the roots growing as they drew up the strength of the earth and circulated it through her body. Day and night she listened to the sound of the roots growing.

In the summer she saw the green water.

In the fall, the cold came. She didn't groan anymore. The roots stopped moving. The growing ceased.

In the winter she was nourished by the dew. She was frozen but she could see the water. Green-blue.

In the spring her entire body was covered with new leaves. It was a good spring. She learned the water's song. When she sang it her heart slowly filled with joy. She gave this joy to the new leaves. The leaves grew greener and greener.

In the summer the water was light blue. She could see the fish.

In the fall, it got cold. The sky was dark. Her heart was full of joy. Her heart had taken on the nature of the tree. She stored everything away.

In midwinter she was nourished by human milk. She had an explosive feeling. Spring hadn't come, but the ice on her body was breaking. She was in pain. She was filled with an explosive feeling. She remained gazing at the water. The water wasn't flowing anymore, it dripped along. The drops were moving and Mahdokht was in pain. Mahdokht was absorbed in the water. In her body she was coming to know the beating heart of every drop. For three months she was nourished by human milk.

In mid-spring the tree in her body exploded. The explosion was not sudden, but rather came slowly. It was as if all the parts of her wanted to separate from each other. The parts of her body separated slowly, groaning. In an eternal metamorphosis the parts of Mahdokht separated from each other. She was in pain, and felt like she was giving birth. Her eyes bulged. The water was no longer in drops. It was ethereal particles and Mahdokht could see them. She opened up along with the ethereal particles of water.

Finally it was finished. The tree had turned completely into seeds. A mountain of seeds. A strong wind blew the seeds of Mahdokht into the water.

Mahdokht traveled with the water. She traveled all over the world.

Faizeh

The air is fresh and pure in the fall. It's nice to go for a walk around eleven o'clock. Every day around eleven Faizeh and Amir went for a walk through the intricate network of alleys of the city.

Every morning Faizeh came from Karaj, and they met each other in Twenty-fourth of Esfand Square. He would complain about his wife and she would listen patiently. The wife was lazy and didn't know how to cook. She couldn't even take care of their baby properly.

Faizeh felt sorry for Amir. She pitied him and gave him advice.

In the middle of the fall, his office penalized him fifteen days' pay for his absences. He was extremely upset, and he changed their meetings to five o'clock in the afternoon.

She came from Karaj every evening to meet Amir

in Twenty-fourth of Esfand Square. They would talk or sometimes go to a movie or a restaurant. It couldn't go on like this. Life was really becoming a bore. They had nothing left to say to each other.

One day Amir said, "Of course I shouldn't be saying this, but it's not good for you to come from Karaj and return every day. I'm afraid that something will happen to you. It's not good for a woman to be coming and going alone on the road to Karaj."

"So what do you think we should do?"

"Come back and live in Tehran."

"In whose house?"

"Go back to your grandmother's house."

"You think she would let me come back? She doesn't understand the way we live, but she thinks that something bad has happened to me, so she would be even nastier than before."

"Maybe it would be better if I rented a room for you."

"Amir, what a rude thing to say. What kind of woman do you think I am?"

"Well, let's make a temporary marriage so that there won't be any problem."

Faizeh didn't like the idea of temporary marriage, but she kept quiet.

One evening they went to a notary public to make a temporary marriage. The notary public said, "We don't do temporary marriages, we do regular marriages." They got married permanently, in secret so that Amir could prepare his wife for the news. That night they went to a hotel.

The morning after the wedding, Amir was upset. He searched in vain for a handkerchief. The girl pretended that she didn't know what was going on. Amir didn't say anything. He just stared out the window. He was extremely unhappy with his luck, and he didn't know who to complain to.

Faizeh said, "We have to look around for a small house."

"Hold off for a while, and I'll take you to my house."

"God forbid! Is that what you think? That I'll come and live with a rival wife? Never!"

Faizeh started looking for a house. She found an attic apartment on Salsabil Street. Amir began to look for a job, and found one in a company. It paid better, so he was able to buy a new house, with the expectation that Faizeh would introduce him to Mr. Aterchiyan.

Their life is neither good nor bad. It just goes on.

Munis

Munis helped the gardener for three months. They fed the tree with Zarrinkolah's milk. In April the tree opened up.

One day they noticed that the tree had been entirely changed into seeds. The wind blew. It spread the seeds to the water.

The gardener said, "Munis, it's time for you to become human."

"I want to become light. How can I become light?"

"By comprehending darkness. Like most people, you don't understand unity. Comprehend darkness. This is the foundation. Don't become light. That's a one-way transformation. Look at your friend, she wanted to become a tree, and she did. It wasn't as difficult as she thought it would be. Unfortunately she didn't become human, she became a tree. Now she can start over so that she can become somewhat human after billions of years. Seek darkness, seek in the darkness, in the beginning, in the depths, in the depths of the depths where you will find light at the zenith, in yourself, by yourself. That is becoming human, go and become human!"

Munis turned around in the blink of an eye and flew off into the sky. A black wind blew her away. She found herself in an endless desert.

Seven years passed, during which she passed through seven deserts. She was tired and thin, and had lost hope. She became filled with experience. That was all there was to it.

After seven years she arrived at the city. She washed herself, put on a clean dress, and became a simple schoolteacher.

Farrokhlaqa Sadraldivan Golchehreh

Farrokhlaqa stayed in the city all winter in the house that she had rented. The painter was at her house almost every day. He was twenty-five years old and full of dreams. He told all of his dreams to Faizeh.

In the fall, there was an exhibit of portraits of Farrokhlaqa from different angles. The opening night was extremely crowded. Everyone came and complimented the work and said, "Wow!" The next day, the exhibit was empty.

The young painter lost his morale. Farrokhlaqa spent the whole winter consoling him. In the beginning of spring, she was tired of his crying and moaning. She gave him money to go to Paris to paint with the masters.

After the artist left, she was alone in the house for a few days. She got bored. She thought about returning to the garden. But she didn't have the patience to put up with the women.

Mr. Marikhi, an old friend of Fakhredin Azad, came to see her. She knew all about his relationship with Fakhredin. She and Mr. Marikhi sat and talked day after day. He respected her. He saw in her an incredible talent that had not been channeled properly.

He suggested that they get married so that he could help Farrokhlaqa do some social climbing. She accepted. They both moved up socially. Marikhi became a representative and Farrokhlaqa dedicated herself to helping the poor. Marikhi received a medal, and Farrokhlaqa became a trustee of an orphanage. Marikhi was stationed in Europe, and Farrokhlaqa went with him.

Their relationship is satisfactory, neither warm nor cold.

Zarrinkolah

Zarrinkolah married the gardener. She got pregnant. She gave birth to a lily. She loved her child, and in a small hole on the riverbank it grew up.

One summer day her husband said, "Zarrinkolah, we must go on a trip."

Zarrinkolah swept the house, wrapped up the bedding, and packed their things.

Her husband said, "Zarrinkolah, we don't need clothes. Leave your bundle here."

She left the bundle and took her husband's hand. They went and sat on the lily together. The lily wrapped them in its petals. They became smoke and rose into the sky.

Afterword

Shahrnush Parsipur belongs to an international tradition of writers who confront the difficulties of writing and publishing in the face of government censorship and harassment. Like many of her contemporaries from Asia, Latin America, the Middle East, and Africa, Parsipur shares the dubious status of being a writer forced into exile because she was unable to write and publish in her homeland. While American writers do not endure such extreme forms of censure and often work under the presumption that they can exercise "free speech" under the First Amendment, a kind of de facto censorship does exist in this country. Writers in the United States contend with an increasingly limited publishing market controlled by a small number of media giants that are gobbling up independent publishers. Owned by some of the most powerful corporations in the media industry (Disney, Rupert Murdoch's News Corp,

AOL Time Warner, Viacom), these publishing companies are concerned with the bottom-line profit margin and are much less willing to take risks on books that deal with more controversial and perhaps less sexy and profitable topics. Over the past two decades, the practice of book-banning in schools and libraries has grown more common in the U.S. as interest groups, usually religious or politically conservative, exert pressure on school boards, libraries, and teachers to limit young people's exposure to controversial and less mainstream literature.

At an important height in her career, Parsipur endured imprisonment, torture, and the banning of all her writing. Unable to make a living as a writer in Iran, she eventually came to the United States in 1994. Until recently, little of Parsipur's work had been translated; thus she has not received the attention she deserves in the English-speaking world. Her novels and short stories shed light on the experiences and sensibilities of modern Iranians, but also challenge American readers to rethink some of the stereotypes and presumptions promulgated in the U.S. media since the 1979 revolution. Parsipur adds an important voice to the international chorus of writers who document, challenge, and artistically represent their society without succumbing to censorship, whether imposed by the government or emanating from inside their own head. The 1998 publication of *Zanan bedun mardan* in its first English-language translation (Women without men) introduced Parsipur to American audiences for the first time. With this critical English-language paperback edition, we hope that Parsipur will begin to reach an even wider audience as an author of international importance whose work is worthy of serious study.

Parsipur wrote *Zanan bedun mardan* over a span of nearly two decades and published it in its current form after the critical success of her novel *Tuba va ma'na-yi shab* (Touba and the meaning of night). The significance of *Women Without Men* may be illustrated best by its continued status as a "banned book" in Iran. The Islamic Republic condemned this book the same year it was first published (1989) and consequently banned it and all of Parsipur's other writings because of the perception that it was un-Islamic and contained unseemly phrases about virginity. The boldness with which she writes about a number of taboo subjects including virginity, rape, prostitution, and resistance to male domination was the principal reason for her two arrests after the book's publication. The stories that constitute *Women Without Men* offer a complex understanding of women's status and position in Iranian society not only in the period after the Iranian Revolution, but also in the decades leading up to the movement that deposed the Shah of Iran in 1979.[1]

Parsipur's censure by her government is neither new in the context of Iran nor across the globe. Throughout Iran's modern history writers have suffered continuous harassment, censure, and even torture and imprisonment. Historically women writers have been underrepresented, not because of the apparatus of state censorship but rather due to self-censorship and because of the social taboos against women participating in public discourses such as writing. Parsipur's plight as a writer is reflected perhaps in the growing trend in nations of the Middle Eastern region where increasingly powerful and aggressive Islamist movements have expressed intolerance with writers they consider to be pro-Western, anti-Islamic, and/or pro-feminist. As women writers have become more visible in Iran and elsewhere, they have experienced censorship, including government harassment and/or government indifference to this harassment.

History

Throughout Iran's tumultuous twentieth-century history, writers of that country have dealt with social and political issues both directly and indirectly in poetry and prose. Under the dictatorial rule of the Pahlavi monarchy (both Reza Shah, who was deposed in 1941, and his son Mohammad Reza Shah, who was ousted during the 1979 revolution), few opportunities were available for organized political opposition. In a society that has little experience with democratic institutions, writing has been one of the principal avenues for expressing social and political criticism and dissent, and for galvanizing political opposition movements. Consequently, many writers of modern Iran have experienced the continuous and heavy hand of censorship—publication of books and articles has been blocked; journals, newspapers, and whole publishing houses have been shut down; books have been banned; and, in the most extreme cases, writers, journalists, and publishers have been imprisoned, tortured, and killed. One need only recall the Ayatollah Khomeini's *fatwa* (Islamic judicial decree) in 1989 that sentenced Salman Rushdie and all those involved in the publication of *The Satanic Verses* to death. Khomeini called on all Muslims to carry out the decree, and placed a $1.5 million bounty on Rushdie's head. This incident drew international attention to Iran's severe censorship practices, but how many lesser-known local writers and journalists have been subject to similarly harsh criticisms and condemnations over the course of Iran's modern history?

While numerous writers have faced prison terms, torture, death, or exile both under the Shah and the current Islamic government, Iran's strong tradition of literature as a voice of consciousness and social criticism has remained forceful and creative. To evade government censors, writers like Shahrnush Parsipur continuously devise strategies to obscure or conceal their critiques. Deploying literary metaphors and allegorical images and language, writers continue to invent ways to protest government policies and actions, and to express dissension. At times, works by these authors are direct and polemical; others are more subtle and perhaps less didactic, but no less powerful or influential.

Prior to the 1979 revolution, few Iranian women writers had readerships and audiences comparable to their male counterparts. Literary production was still a discursive realm dominated by men, and few women writers could transcend the social stigma suffered by women who assume this public role. Instead, women frequently were confined to the private and more modest realms of the domestic sphere. The veil, an extension of Islamic ideas of virtue, chastity, and modesty, has functioned as a factor in limiting women's public visibility and bodily significance.

It is also symbolic of the limitations on women's intellectual and political participation. The veil has been an important, albeit controversial, icon for Iranian national identity; at various points in Iranian history it was voluntarily worn by many women, then outlawed under Reza Shah in 1936, and then reinstituted as compulsory after the establishment of the Islamic Republic.[2] In addition to the physical experience of veiling, Iranian women still contend with the Iranian concept of *sharm,* a difficult term to translate that loosely connotes rules and behavior expected of women to maintain their "reputation." Sharm governs standards of femininity, beauty, modesty, self-restraint, and, ultimately, a woman's sense of sexual comportment and obedience. The social ideas associated with sharm and notions of the "ideal woman" have been historically a barrier to women's public expression (Milani 53). Often women writers still practice their own de facto form of self-censorship as a response to the attitudes condemning women's public expression. Farzaneh Milani connects this self-censorship not only with the generally small number of texts written and published by women, but even more dramatically in the genre of autobiography, where a kind of self-revelation is necessary:

> Seen within this context the rare attempts at autobiography found in contemporary Iran are the logical literary extension of a culture that creates, expects, and values a sharply defined separation between the inner and the outer, the private and the public. They indicate strong forces of deindividualization, protection, and repression. Concealing, keeping the private *private,* is not just a matter of veiling and not just a woman's problem. It seems to be a relative constant of Persian experience (Milani 215).

The history of women's authorship and writing in Iran is deeply connected to attitudes about women's education and the threat that women pose if they question, challenge, or voice their opposition to Iran's deeply patriarchal system. While women experienced some social reforms and educational advancement in Iran under the reign of the Pahlavis, the essential attitude toward women held by the two Shahs remained the same: they had little regard for women's ability to contribute socially and politically beyond their domestic roles as wives and mothers. While some writers (like Forough Farrokhzad, the famous twentieth-century poet) were able to establish themselves as writers with a significant literary following, most women writers were marginal to the largely male literary world and were often criticized more harshly than their male counterparts.

After the 1979 revolution, Ayatollah Khomeini imposed new laws requiring women to once again wear the veil (*hejab*). Ironically, this institutionalized oppression reinvigorated the struggle by women for a modicum of equality, and more women began to write, publish, and rebel against their "silencing" than ever before. Shahrnush Parsipur associates the proliferation of women's writing after the revolution with women's dramatic awakening to their oppression: "When the government suddenly decided that it could and would humiliate women," said Parsipur, "these same women understood their condition like never before. For them, the only opportunity to rise up was with their words. I believe that women writers have found a way to become political through writing."[3] Parsipur does not see herself as a political activist and eschews any association with organized political movements, including feminism:

> I am not a feminist. But I am not against feminism either. I think some forms of feminism are too extreme. I believe women have had to be preoccupied with notions such as virginity, and it has been a real barrier

> to their spiritual and intellectual progress. They have not been able to express themselves politically; that's my concern for Iranian women and what some of my works touch upon.

Parsipur's desire to not be labeled with any particular political party or movement points to her decision to distinguish herself from earlier literary movements that were decidedly politically "committed" or what was termed *"engagé"* (didactic or political) writing in Iran. Parsipur's writing, ironically, has a very real political affect among her readers and has led to her own politicization as writer.

Biography

The daughter of an attorney in the Justice Ministry, Shahrnush Parsipur was born in Tehran, Iran, in 1946. At an early age, Parsipur showed an interest in literature, and her liberal-minded parents encouraged her education and supported her interest in writing. At the age of eleven or twelve she read a translation of Fyodor Dostoyevsky's *The Insulted and Injured* and was deeply moved by the experience. She read every novel by Dostoyevsky and has said that each one of them influenced her: "Dostoyevsky is a deeply psychological writer and he understands something about the spiritual nature of human beings." As she grew into her teen years, Parsipur voraciously read literature from Russia and Europe. She was particularly taken with Charles Dickens and read *Great Expectations* a total of thirty times. Because she wrote well and received praise for her school compositions, Parsipur felt destined for a career in writing. Although there existed few models for her to emulate in Iran (very few Iranian women were actively writing and even fewer were being published), Parsipur enthusiastically pursued her love of writing. At the age of sixteen she published her first short story. As she developed her craft, Parsipur began to search for role models. Rather than drawing inspiration from a small and lesser-known group of women writers, Parsipur found her greatest inspiration in the modernist Iranian writer Sadeq Hedayat (1903–1951), author of the internationally acclaimed *The Blind Owl,* as well as a number of European and American writers including Charles Dickens, Franz Kafka, Mark Twain, and Ernest Hemingway.

After graduating from high school, Parsipur entered the University of Tehran among the first women to be admitted. Because the disciplinary choices available to women were limited (they were obliged to take courses in the evening), Parispur decided to pursue her bachelor's degree in sociology because it combined her interests in social and historical issues and enabled her to continue to write. During her university years, Parsipur published several short stories including *Tupak-i qermez* (The little red ball) and *Garma dar sal-i sefr* (Heat in the year zero). A number of her short stories were published in popular Iranian literary journals, including the well-known journal *Jong-e Esfahan.* Her novella *Tajrubah'ha-yi azad* (Trial offers, 1970) was followed by her first novel, *Sag va zimistan-i boland* (The dog and the long winter, 1974). A collection of short stories called *Avizah'ha-yi bulur* (Crystal pendants) was published in 1977.

It was during her studies at the University of Tehran that Parsipur became fascinated with Chinese philosophy. After reading a book on Chinese astrology, Parsipur was introduced by an American friend to a professor at the Royal Institute of Philosophy who taught a course on *I Ching.* Sensing Parsipur's growing passion for Chinese philosophy, Professor Izutsu (originally from Japan) encouraged her to study Chinese to gain direct access to Chinese writing. While attending university, she also worked as a producer for Iranian National Television and Radio, a position from which she resigned in 1974 in protest of the execution of two poets by the Shah's regime. Shortly thereafter, she was arrested by the Shah's intelligence agency, SAVAK, and imprisoned for a short period. In 1976, she traveled to France to attend the Sorbonne, where she continued her studies of Chinese language and culture. During her four-year stay in Paris she completed her second book, *Majara-ha-yi sadah va kuchak-i ruh-i dirakht* (The simple and small adventures of the tree spirit), an erotic novel that continues the story of a character in *The Dog and the Long Winter*. The novel was published by an Iranian publisher in Sweden twenty years after she wrote it.

During the tumult of the Iranian Revolution, Parsipur interrupted her studies and decided to return to Iran. She was very interested in the role women had played in the revolution and in seeing the outcome of this popular movement against the former Shah. But shortly after her return from Paris in 1980, she found herself arrested and imprisoned without ever having any formal charges made against her. Her arrest took place in 1981, a time when the new government was cracking down on all opposition groups in an attempt to consolidate power and specifically in response to the Mohajjedin, an organization that had declared its opposition to the new regime. Parsipur describes her arrest and the arrest of her mother and brothers as the result of her brother's attempt to create an archive of political publications. Parsipur was initially held at Evin prison and then later transferred to Qazalhassar. She spent a total of four years, seven months, and seven days in prison:

> My prison term was particularly lengthy because I protested the cruelty that was inflicted on me and my fellow prisoners. They wanted to destroy the humanity of the prisoners, and they sought to do this with cruel punishment and by forcing a kind of re-education on us that was intended to break our spirits.

While Parsipur was not affiliated with any political group, she, like many of the thousands of women who were arrested and detained during this period, was made an example of due to her outspokenness and apparently non-conformist behavior. In particular, Parsipur was beaten or ostracized at times for improper hejab, for not praying, and for speaking her mind. In her *Khatirat-i zandan* (Prison memoirs, 1996), she recounts one incident where she was banned from speaking with anyone except her mother for having voiced concern about environmental destruction resulting from the ongoing war with Iraq. Many of Parsipur's fellow inmates were a generation younger than she, and a majority of them were students. Parsipur had little opportunity to write and read in prison: "What books we did have access to were religious books. It was only in my last year of imprisonment that I was allowed to read anything other than religious material."

Once Parsipur was released from prison in 1986, she faced the problem of having no money and little chance of finding work in the repressive climate of the mid-1980s. "I wanted to get back to writing, and to make some money. I decided to open a bookshop but had to close it after six months because the Revolutionary Guards were coming around and wanting to know who was visiting the store," said Parsipur. Facing difficult economic circumstances, Parsipur found piecemeal work translating books and architectural journal articles, as well as writing an occasional book review for literary journals.

By 1989, Parsipur had found a publisher for *Tuba va ma'na-yi shab* (Touba and the meaning of night). The novel was published to widespread acclaim and became a national best-seller. *Touba* narrates the story of a young girl who comes of age and matures over a period of several decades in Iran's tumultuous late nineteenth-century history. Like the historical figure Tahereh Qorratol'Ayn—a woman who was executed in 1852 at the age of thirty-six for presumably being a heretic and a promoter of the Babi faith—the fictional Touba stands out because she is taught to read and write by her own father. After her father's death, Touba assumes the responsibilities of the household, since she is the only literate member of the family. At the age of fourteen, she proposes marriage to her father's fifty-two-year old uncle, who has assumed the household's financial responsibilities. Her husband does not treat her respectfully and is threatened by Touba's intelligence, beauty, and outspokenness (Nooriala 141). The real life of Tahereh Qorratol'Ayn is surrounded by mystery and silence, but one of the important reasons that Parsipur has claimed her in *Touba* is because she was literate, educated, and outspoken, "the first challenge to an age-old, male-centered, male-dominated belief system" (Milani 98). The use of the historical figure Tahereh in this novel contributed in part to its controversial reception. While Tahereh was considered a heretic for both her religious beliefs and for her ability to speak and write eloquently on topics and issues that were the exclusive domain of men, Parsipur portrays her as a woman coming to consciousness about her own oppression as a woman. The novel also portrays Touba as venturing into "orthodox religion, Sufism, nationalism, and other forms of thought only to find them futile" (Talattof 144). Even while the novel was very popular, both the depiction of Touba as a writer/critic of male discourse and her exploration into the world of religion would not sit comfortably with the Islamic Republic and would, by Parsipur's own admission, draw negative attention to the author.

In addition to *Touba's* content, Parsipur's writing style in this novel was a departure from previous pre-revolutionary writing, which either deployed a straightforward social-realist style or an allegorical and often political message. Two of the main characters come from ancient times to the present, and the novel employs Parsipur's use of the fantastic as well as a shifting sense of narrative time. In *Women Without Men,* some of the characters die and return to life, disappear, or transform into other essences—trees, wind, smoke. While some readers and critics connect Parsipur's writing to the magical-realist tradition, Parsipur suggests that this literary phenomenon is homegrown and predates authors like Gabriel García Marquez and Isabel Allende who have made it popular in the Latin American context. "This type of writing is not borrowed from Latin America, but is something that originates in this part of the world. If you just read *The Thousand and One Nights,* you'll see where I and other authors derive inspiration for the use of the fantastic, the unexplainable," said Parsipur. In addition to this fantastic, non-linear narrative style that has become her trademark, Parsipur's work has consistently shown a concern with women's oppression and the limitations placed on women by patriarchal society. While Parsipur expresses some discomfort with being labeled a feminist writer, it is hard to miss a certain feminist sensibility in her writing that questions and challenges male privilege and the institutions and ideologies that reinforce it.

Despite *Touba*'s controversial depiction of women, Parsipur was able to get it published. *Women Without Men,* however, was far more radical. After the 1989 publication of *Touba* brought her some notoriety, she finally found a publisher willing to take a chance on her novella. Although the stories from *Women Without Men* were written mostly before the revolution (and several had been published as individual stories before the novella took its final form), it was while she was in Paris watching the revolution unfold that Parsipur found the thread that joined the five narratives together in the space of the garden in Karaj. *Women Without Men* proved to be far too radical in its critique of male patriarchy, and while it brought her success, it also prompted the government to arrest her two more times; on both occasions she was jailed for more than a month:

> Their chief goal was to intimidate me because they couldn't do much else. After the critical success of *Touba,* they didn't know what to do with me. So they harassed me, told me to desist from such writing and they attacked the man who published the book.

Mohammad Reza Aslani, the publisher and owner of Noghreh Publishing, was also arrested, and his publishing house was immediately closed down. The charge leveled against Parsipur was that she had written about virginity in the novella and had too forcefully broached a taboo subject. Apparently *Women Without Men* was also perceived as un-Islamic because of references to Western culture. One of the book's characters refers to *The Sound of Music* and *Gone with the Wind;* another character is compared to the actress Vivien Leigh. "After the publication of *Women Without Men,*" said Parsipur, "all my books were banned and I immediately confronted the same difficult circumstances I faced after getting out of prison. I did not have the ability to make a living as a writer."

Ironically, Parsipur's success and consequent condemnation in Iran allowed her to travel abroad and speak out about the difficulties of living in a repressive and censorial society. Parsipur's other publications include her novels

Aql-i abi (Blue wisdom, 1994), *Shiva* (1999), and *Bar bal-i bad neshastan* (Sitting on the wings of the wind, 2002). Parsipur has also published another collection of short stories, *Adab-i sarf-i chai dar huzur-i gorg* (Tea ceremony in the presence of wolves, 1993). One of her novellas, *Tajrubah'ha-yi azad* (Trial offers) has been published in *Stories from Iran: A Chicago Anthology* (1992). In addition to her short stories and novels, Parsipur has written many articles and essays for literary journals published in Iran, the United States, and Europe.

In the early 1990s, Parsipur traveled to the United States, Canada, and Europe. After returning from a year abroad, however, Parsipur found life in Iran stressful and difficult. When she was invited back to the United States in 1994, she decided to stay and seek refugee status. She has been living in the San Francisco Bay Area since then.

The Novel

While the five narrative voices of *Women Without Men* are straightforward, the ideas they convey are far from simple. The series of narratives weaves together the fates of five different women in the garden in Karaj, which becomes a kind of utopic space where women live together without men. The novella's title is a play on Ernest Hemingway's collection of short stories *Men Without Women,* and admittedly Parsipur suggests that she is up to something similar. "I read Hemingway's collection and found that he wanted to show that men had no sense without women. They couldn't touch the feminine spirit," she said. Parsipur states that her intention in this novel is to draw attention to some of the fallacies that are the foundation of male supremacy in Iranian culture, including the idea of virginity. "Women have sexual desire and the idea of virginity impedes them from expressing that desire. Women are only allowed to express their sexuality in the context of marriage, and the obsession with virginity is *ridiculous,*" said Parsipur.

The opening story of "Mahdokht" leads readers to see the internalized oppression of young women and the consequences of a society's preoccupation with virginity. Mahdokht, a young woman who loves children, finds herself knitting sweaters for her brother's children and wanting to perform charitable acts for other children. She compares herself to Maria, the character in the musical *The Sound of Music:* "'I am just like Julie,' she thought" (4). Mahdokht compares her love of children and her compassion for small and vulnerable things with Julie Andrews's character Maria. What Mahdokht fails to see in the comparison is the fact that Julie Andrews (Maria) is a nun taking care of someone else's children. In the act of being a governess who later marries her male employer, the wealthy Austrian widower, she transgresses against the church, the convent, and her commitment to a life of chastity. In Mahdokht's telling of the story, however, "Julie decided to marry the Austrian, since she was carrying his eighth child" (4). When Mahdokht witnesses a sexual act between the gardener, Yadallah, and a fifteen-year-old girl in the garden's greenhouse, Mahdokht becomes horrified and disgusted. She does not know what to do. The girl begs Mahdokht not to tell her mother and says that the gardener wants to marry her. Mahdokht promises not to tell anyone, but secretly hopes the girl becomes pregnant so that her brothers will kill her. "How good that would be," Mahdokt thinks to herself (10). Mahdokht turns this episode of unbridled sexual desire between this young girl and Yadallah into a lesson for herself: "'My virginity is like a tree,' she thought suddenly" (10). Mahdokht decides that she must stay in the garden and "plant herself" in the ground. Mahdokht's desire to transform into a tree becomes a metaphor for the fulfillment of her sexual desire without the loss of her virginity—an act she dreads and fears. At the end of the novel, Mahdokht sprouts roots, grows, gets new leaves, and finally turns into a mountain of seeds that is spread across the world. She thus propagates herself without engaging in the messy business of human sexuality.

"Faizeh," the second story in the novella, introduces readers to a character whose narrative takes place in August 1953—the same month that Mohammad Mossadeq, the former prime minister of Iran, was overthrown in a U.S.-backed coup d'état. The setting and tone of the story is made clear from the first few sentences:

> At four o'clock in the afternoon on the twenty-fifth of August, 1953, after days of hesitation Faizeh made her decision. Silence no longer had any meaning. Had she waited any longer, everything would have fallen apart. She had to go and defend her rights. (13)

Which rights Faizeh is going to defend is not completely clear. Is it her right to move about the city in the ensuing melee that characterized Tehran after the August 16 coup d'état? Is it her right not to be told how to cook Western food? Is it her right not to be silenced by her sister-in-law Parvin, who accuses Faizeh of not protecting her virginity? Is it her right to exercise her political views about the situation taking place in Iran? By framing the story in the period of the U.S.-backed coup, Parsipur suggests that women were not politically engaged because they were preoccupied instead with activities such as gossiping and monitoring one another's sexual and social behavior. More specifically, the story points to the culturally-determined preoccupation of women with their "reputation" and ultimately their sexual purity.

Faizeh's narrative directs readers to one of the most controversial aspects of the novella and the reason for Parsipur's persecution by the Iranian government. In this chapter, while defending herself against Parvin's allegations of her sexual impurity, Faizeh informs her sister-in-law that "virginity is not a curtain, it's a hole" (26). By confronting her sister-in-law with this truth she names the very thing Parvin makes inferences to but cannot publicly state. But Faizeh takes her insult one step further: "You've had three kids and you still don't know that it's a hole, not a curtain. And then you spread rumors about people" (26). The fact of Faizeh's naming and exposing the thing that threatened to damage her empowers Faizeh against her sister-in-law. She not only refuses the accusation made against her reputation, she calls Parvin ignorant and ridicules her lack of understanding of her own body. Faizeh claims knowledge about the physical presence of virginity by saying that she has "read about it in a book"

(27). Reading empowers Faizeh to repel the allegation and insult by another woman, but it does not empower her beyond that. She is far from intellectual, and even buys into the theory that round-faced women, like her friend Munis, are stupid.

Munis is far from stupid. She is curious and interested in what is happening around her. In the chapter titled "Faizeh" we first encounter Munis attentively listening to the radio when Faizeh approaches her. While Munis is interested in the events taking shape during the days of the coup, it is obvious from her brother's statement to Faizeh that "home is for women, the outside world is for men" (28) and that Munis lives a sheltered life. It is when Faizeh tells Munis that virginity is a hole and not a curtain (as her mother had taught her) that something inside her unravels and she is filled with rage:

> Munis thought about how for thirty-eight years she had been looking out the window at the little garden, assuming that virginity was a curtain. When she was eight years old, they had told her that God would never forgive a girl who lost her virginity. Now it had been three days and two nights since she found out that virginity is a hole, not a curtain. (29)

Munis recalls her childhood memory of longingly looking at a tree, but choosing not to climb it because she feared it would "tear" the curtain of her virginity. Her rage at the lie perpetuated by her family sends her out onto the chaotic and dangerous streets of Tehran following the coup, where she decides to "take revenge." Against her brother's specific instructions not to go out, Munis leaves the house and spends a month walking the streets, observing the "outside" world. Finally, she ends up at a bookstall where she purchases a book titled *The Secret of Sexual Satisfaction or How to Know Our Bodies.* Munis uses her act of reading to "grow up" and to reclaim her body and her mind, and to transform herself. When she returns home, however, she is confronted by the servant Alia and her brother, Amir, both of whom are distressed at seeing her return seemingly happy and of her own free will. In a fit of rage, her brother accuses her of ruining the family reputation, assuming, of course, that she has lost her virginity. When she asks him why he is so upset, he reaches for a knife and stabs her to death. The scene conjures the notion of honor killing (whereby male relatives feel justified in killing their sisters/daughters for their bringing shame on the family), and Parsipur identifies Amir with the irrational and total investment that Iranian men, particularly male relatives, often have in policing women's bodies and their sexual purity.

Faizeh's complicity in hiding this murderous act by Munis's brother also suggests the ease with which women also cooperate with male violence against women. In Munis's murder, Faizeh sees an opportunity to get closer to Amir. After Faizeh and Amir hide Munis's body in the garden, she suggests that it is a good time for Amir to get married because it will draw attention away from the missing Munis. But instead of taking this as a hint about Faizeh's own availability, Amir seeks out a much younger virgin to marry. He describes the girl as "very beautiful, soft and quiet, modest, shy, kind, diligent, hard-working, dignified, chaste, elegant, and neat. She wears a chador, always looks down when she's in the street, and blushes constantly" (41). This description is a litany of characteristics that compose the timeless description of an "ideal" Iranian woman: chaste, modest, and silent. Parsipur's use of such a description is of course ironic and points to the prison that this silence and chastity creates for all women. When Munis arises from her grave in the garden, she is alive again with a new ability to read minds. She seeks revenge a second time by exposing Amir's bride's secret on their wedding night, proving that the eighteen-year-old woman is not a virgin but had had an abortion the previous year after getting pregnant by her cousin. Munis's return from the dead and her ability to read minds is part of her transformation and her revenge against the lies that have been told to her.

In these two short stories, Parsipur exposes a tangled web of ignorance, complicity, and duplicity surrounding virginity and the need to control and police women's sexuality. It is this need for control that destroys relationships between men and women, and among women, and ultimately limits women's capacity to grow and develop as full human beings. Parsipur's interest in locating some of her stories during the coup d'état against Mossadeq was, she said, intended to show the "spiritual condition of Iranian women at a time when the society was in crisis." According to Parsipur, during the coup some women had political ideas, but other women were caught up in gossip and in monitoring other women's "reputations." Parsipur shows readers how limited, in fact, women's political participation was. Iranian women after the revolution, however, were far more engaged and vocal. They took to the streets in large numbers in the effort to overthrow the Shah, and when Ayatollah Khomeini called for a return to the veil, they vehemently protested. "Today women want to participate and they keep trying and trying, but there are so many institutions and ideologies blocking them," said Parsipur.

In "Mrs. Farrokhlaqa Sadraldivan Golchehreh," Parsipur draws another depiction of male control and dominance over women. Farrokhlaqa, the only married woman we encounter in the first five stories, is a fifty-year-old woman who is suffocated by her husband's domineering presence. Golchehreh, her husband of thirty years, is obviously insecure and needs to control his wife. He keeps a constant surveying eye on her and allows her little emotional or spiritual space. He is simultaneously drawn to and threatened by her beauty. Not knowing how to love his wife, Golchehreh can relate to her only by doling out criticism and ridiculing her in order to make himself feel better. Rather than focusing on virginity and women's reputation, this chapter takes another aspect of women's sexuality, menopause, as the focus of Parsipur's criticism of patriarchal control. Golchehreh repeatedly comments to his wife that soon she will be entering menopause and will be incapable of "enjoying a garden." Golchehreh does not know how to respect or talk to her; the only way he sees her is through the sexual frames provided by his culture. Farrokhlaqa's memories of Fakhredine, the man who truly loved and respected her (before she married) and who equates her beauty with that of the glamorous American actress Vivien Leigh, give her an escape from the tension and boredom of her marriage. One day when Golchehreh is looking at her in a strange way, without the habitual resentment and derision of the past thirty years, she becomes frightened. She assumes that he is planning something, perhaps even to kill her. In a moment of suspicion, she punches him in the stomach and accidentally kills him. In her husband's death she finds freedom and pursues her dream of purchasing a garden in Karaj.

Zarrinkolah, the fifth character, is an experienced prostitute who one day becomes troubled by the continuous experience of seeing her many customers as headless. She is afraid that if she tells someone that she sees all the men in the brothel without their heads, they will think she is crazy or possessed by demons. Instead, she keeps this experience to herself and tells only one person, the innocent new girl who comes to work at the brothel. The two women vow to tell each other if they see the customers as headless. Zarrinkolah continues to see the men without heads, but her younger friend sees all the men with heads. The young girl suggests that Zarrinkolah pray and make some sort of vow. The fact of Zarrinkolah's portrayal as a prostitute would seem controversial enough. But she is also portrayed with a great deal of humanity and is well-liked by her fellow sex-workers; naturally, she is ill-treated by Akram Seven, the brothel owner who regularly beats her. Zarrinkolah's identity is more or less fixed as a prostitute until the headless customers start appearing. This encourages Zarrinkolah to find a way out of her predicament. She decides to go to a public bathhouse, gets a private bath, and has a bathworker scrub so hard her skin feels raw. She asks the bathworker how to perform ablutions and suddenly experiences an urge to pray. She prays naked in the bathhouse and prostrates herself while calling out the name Ali, the first and most important Imam in Shi'i Islam. Parsipur's depiction of a prostitute performing ablutions, then praying naked to Ali, might also have been unnerving to the Islamic government. Zarrinkolah finds something redeeming in her ritual cleansing and acts of prayer. Her fate is no longer that of a prostitute. She finds a destiny for herself: she will go to the garden in Karaj.

After the unfortunate death of Farrokhlaqa's husband, she purchases a garden in Karaj, specifically the former garden of Mahdokht's family wherein Mahdokht decided to plant herself and become a human tree. Rather than finding disgrace in the idea of a human tree, Farrokhlaqa begins to think it will bring her fame and ultimately enable her to fulfill her dream of being a parliamentary representative. Farrokhlaqa decides to add rooms to the house and creates a kind of women's shelter for the four other women who end up in Karaj. Here they pass the time, take care of the garden (and Mahdokht the tree), and entertain guests. For each of the five women, the garden becomes a symbol of their freedom from male control and their capacity to reinvent themselves outside the confines of male society. Farrokhlaqa acts as a kind of patron/mother-figure who enables the younger women to live independently in a utopic women's space.

On their way to the garden, however, Faizeh and Munis are stopped by two men driving a truck. When they ask the women where they are going, Faizeh answers that they are on their way "to Karaj to reap the benefits of our toil and get rid of the men who control us" (78). The two men laugh and then proceed to rape Munis and Faizeh. Munis does not appear to be as traumatized by the rape as her friend because she has "already died twice" and thus sees things quite differently. Although she is violated and presumably loses her virginity, she does not view it as important: "Well, Faizeh dear, I was a virgin too. To hell with it. We were virgins, now we're not. It's nothing to cry over"

(97). While the narrative somewhat minimizes the violation, Parsipur focuses on the fact that the taking of the two women's virginity is not essential to their success or happiness in life. Munis's revelation and transformation after reading the book on sexuality makes her see the rape as a spiritual obstacle to be overcome that will merely strengthen and teach her.

The gardener, who had been a passenger in the truck of the two men who committed the rape, calls himself the "good gardener" (presumably in contrast with the gardener who has a sexual encounter with the young girl in the greenhouse) and is hired to work in Farrokhlaqa's new garden. He is the only male who works in and nurtures the garden and the one man who forges a bond with the women. He later marries Zarrinkolah and impregnates her. The gardener and Zarrinkolah become Mahdokht's guardians, feeding her with morning dew. When Zarrinkolah becomes pregnant they also administer breast milk to the tree. At the end of the novella, Zarrinkolah give birth, not a child but to a beautiful lily, which the couple plants on the riverbank.

While the garden in Karaj serves as temporary refuge for each of the women in their quest for some form of freedom and spiritual transformation, it is not their final destination. The garden serves as a space for the women to be at home and to be in a kind of secluded domesticity, but none of them is satisfied living a life separate from the outside world or a life without men. Some characters, like Mahdokht and Munis, transcend the limitations of their human body; the protected and nurturing space of the garden facilitates this. For others, like Zarrinkolah and Farrokhlaqa, the garden enables them to reimagine their relationship to the world and hence to men. They are able to choose relationships based on love and respect and fulfill some of their own needs.

In *Women Without Men,* Parsipur seems to suggest that while these women initially live with the oppression of men, living completely isolated without men is not the answer either. While much of the emphasis in Iran was on the explicit utterances of virginity, some readers (including those in the government) seem to have missed the subtlety with which she raises issues of women's spiritual and psychological existence. Parsipur gives us a much more complex understanding of women by denying us simple or romantic answers. For while these characters all end up leaving the garden (some by physically leaving and others by transcending their human bodies), the reader is left not with a simplistic argument (one that Parsipur would naturally find extreme) that the world or women would be better off without men. Indeed, Parsipur leaves us with the idea that for women to be fully human they must step outside some of the limiting and oppressive frames established by a patriarchal society and create their own terms for their identity. To do this, they must not simply exist or act in reaction against that society. They must find their own inner voices guided by their psychological visions of what is possible.

The Writer in Exile

Living in exile in the United States has proven to be a challenge for Parsipur. "I miss my audience, the audience of my people, my language, my culture. Here, I am always between audiences. Here, in exile, I live an isolated life," says Parsipur. Although Parsipur was able to write *Prison Memoirs* since seeking exile in the United States, health problems have made writing more difficult in recent years. Her influence on a younger generation of Iranian women writers, however, has been profound. Many younger writers, intellectuals, and activists admire her ability to artfully tackle difficult gender issues and to expose the hypocrisy and oppression of patriarchal culture. "I believe that my work has influenced younger women and has made them responsible. In a sense, I have shown women that writing is indeed a way to be political," said Parsipur.

Although Parsipur's writing continues to be banned in Iran, underground copies of her books continue to be circulated and read in that society. Several of her novels and short stories have been translated into English, German, French, and Italian. In this country and Europe, she continues to be sought out for lectures, writing residencies, and teaching workshops. During the 2003–2004 academic year Parsipur was designated Brown University's first International Writing Fellow for the Program in Creative Writing and the Watson Institute for International Studies. The fellowship is designed to provide support for established creative writers–fiction writers, playwrights, and poets–who find it difficult to practice free expression in their home countries. Shirin Neshat, the internationally acclaimed video and installation artist, is currently working on a film adaptation of *Women Without Men* in Morocco. "It's a very beautiful story with a political message about the exiled community and ideas of utopia," says Neshat in an interview in *Resistance,* "and yet it's very poetic and mystical, and very feminist. It's also very Iranian, but it's not about Iran" (9).

Women Without Men presents Western readers with an opportunity to read and study the work of an important writer whose oeuvre is shaping a generation of writers in the Iranian context, and whose plight as a banned writer participates in a longstanding global tradition of authors evoking controversial ideas that are threatening to established governments and ideologies. *Women Without Men* can be read and studied in a number of contexts within college and university classrooms. It can be read in world literature classrooms as an example of contemporary Iranian literature; in Middle Eastern studies courses as an example of the way literature addresses women's issues; in courses that deal with censorship and book banning; and in women's studies courses that address the various ways feminist discourses are articulated outside the European and American contexts. This novella can also be used in comparative literature classrooms that take up various relationships between writers and their literary predecessors, and the ways that writers articulate the powerful influence of cultural transmission from one cultural context to another—from east to west and west to east.

While we eagerly await more translations of Parsipur's work, we also await more of the writing that she produces in exile. The hardship and pain of exile is profound in the life of a writer. But exile also produces interesting and innovative sources for creativity. Parsipur's reflections on her life as a writer facing arrest, torture, and imprisonment have been documented in *Prison Memoirs* (as yet not available in English) and offer clues about the ways a tumultuous event such as a revolution can impact the culture of a nation and its literary figures. Moreover, reading Iranian literature can illuminate for American readers, both now and in the future, the rich and complex culture and society of Iran. In reading *Women Without Men,* we can inaugurate a more sophisticated encounter with Iranian literature and culture, and perhaps shed light on issues that are too often left to headlines. As history suggests, literature is a powerful force through which we find our human connections and begin to foster understanding, and hopefully, create a dialogue that stands outside the realm of governmental policies and agendas.

Persis M. Karim
Berkeley, California
2003

NOTES

1. While the story of the Iranian Revolution of 1979 is complicated, it can best be summarized as a populist revolution brought on by the convergence of a number of experiences, events, and trends. From 1947 until his demise in 1979, Mohammad Reza Shah ruled as a dictatorial monarch, disallowing political opposition and actively repressing (including the use of torture and imprisonment) his detractors. While some social and economic

reforms were made under his leadership in the 1960s, the Shah ultimately ruled with an iron fist. The rising expectations of the oil boom in the early 1970s, a large and highly educated middle class, disaffected workers in the oil industry, an increasingly repressive police apparatus (the SAVAK were a CIA-trained organization), and a religious elite that saw its power being greatly eroded by the Shah and his pro-Western policies all contributed to the sentiment that it was time to overthrow the Pahlavi dynasty. The revolution is often described as one of the most effective populist movements of the twentieth century, and succeeded in overthrowing the Shah in a very short time. The revolution, which originally set out to remove the Shah, became quickly "Islamicized" when the exiled mullah Ayatollah Khomeini returned, after fourteen years in exile in France, in 1979 and became one of the leaders of the movement. Within a year, the revolution's agenda and tone had shifted from a movement to depose the Shah to an all-out power grab by opposition groups vying for the future of Iranian leadership. In the end, the Islamist elements succeeded (by forcing out some of the liberal elements), and by 1981 the government of the Islamic Republic of Iran was securely established with the Islamic clergy sitting at the helm of the new nation. The Islamicization of all aspects of Iranian life was fully set in motion by year's end.

2. The veil has been a potent symbol in discourses surrounding religion and national identity throughout Iran's modern history. It has also, in my opinion, been over-determined in discussions of the Middle East and women's issues in that part of the world, often obscuring or distorting women's agency and resistance. A number of important scholarly works on gender, the veil, and Islam have been written including *Women and Gender in Islam* by Leila Ahmed and *Beyond the Veil* by Fatima Mernissi.

3. All quotes by Shahrnush Parsipur, unless otherwise indicated, are from an interview by the author of this afterword held on July 24, 2003, in Albany, California.

4. Several chapters of Parsipur's *Prison Memoirs* were translated into English in Zjaleh Hajibashi's unpublished dissertation (University of Texas at Austin, 1998).

5. Farzaneh Milani, *Veils and Words: The Emerging Voices of Iranian Women Writers,* Syracuse: Syracuse University Press, 1992, 6. In Persian, the term *parde-ye bekarat* can be translated as "the virginity curtain," which would be "the hymen" in English.

7. *Touba and the Meaning of Night* will be published in its first English-language translation by the Feminist Press in 2004.

8. *Resistance,* July/August 2003, 6:4.

WORKS CITED AND RECOMMENDED BIBLIOGRAPHY

Ahmed, Leila. *Women and Gender in Islam.* New Haven: Yale University Press, 1992.

Mernissi, Fatima. *Beyond the Veil.* Cambridge: Schenkman, 1975.

Milani, Farzaneh. *The Emerging Voices of Iranian Women Writers.* Syracuse: Syracuse University Press, 1992.

Nooriala, Partow. "Parsipur's *Touba and the Meaning of Night:* A Synopsis." In *Exiles and Explorers: Iranian Diaspora Literature Since 1980.* Ed. Ardavan Davaran. Special issue of *The Literary Review* 40:1 (fall 1996): 141–146.

Parsipur, Shahrnush. *Women Without Men.* Trans. Kamran Talattof and Jocelyn Sharlet. Syracuse: Syracuse University Press, 1998; New York: Feminist Press, 2004.

Talattof, Kamran. *The Politics of Writing in Iran: A History of Modern Persian Literature.* Syracuse: Syracuse University Press, 2000.

Translating Context: A Translator's Note

Shahrnush Parsipur published *Zanan bedun mardan* (Women without men) in 1989 in Tehran. The first English-language translation appeared in the United States in 1998, issued by Syracuse University Press, now available in a critical edition by the Feminist Press. The book was published in Iran amidst a set of cultures and environments new to the author and her readers. Post-revolutionary Iran was a period in time and space of tremendous change in the country's modern history, when women's bodies once again became the negotiation site between the forces of tradition and modernity. Women began anew their struggle to defend their most basic rights in the face of an ideological apparatus that believed controlling women's bodies would combat societal corruption.

The 1979 revolution brought to power a new elite whose ideology stressed religion as the most important organizing principle of society. This revolution and its subsequent sociopolitical changes, the compulsory dress code that followed, and the women's demonstration against mandatory veiling in March 1979 provide important context for the observed shift in women's literature and the subsequent creation of what many now consider a feminist literary discourse, one in which I would argue Parsipur played a decisive role (Talattof 1997).

Our decision to produce a translation through which the sociopolitical paradigm and its discursive power in *Women Without Men* would be meaningful to readers in a different time and cultural setting was based on the belief that some of the book's basic themes—including underlying cultural assumptions and problems around gender—hold universal relevance. However, to translate or transfer such complexities through a guest language means conveying not only words, metaphors, and indications but also the intonations and verbal twists that always add meaning to syntax and to the text's message in the original language. The combination of these elements and the author's innovative use of language in breaking taboos about sexuality provided ample incentive to translate this novel.

Is the oral speech audible in the English version? Perhaps yes. Women's common experience in the face of social limitation helps the characters' voices be heard across the impediment of translation. A sarcastic tone, an angry response, or a scream may be easily distinguished, even in literal translation.

To be sure, the novel's five women converge in a country garden in Karaj where they have a chance to address their problems in new ways. The garden is a green, wooded land with a flowing river, a place of hope. Yet it is also a locus of fantasy, a place nonexistent except in this utopic literary space, which alludes to the allegorical garden of paradise in Persian and Islamic traditions. The garden provides a forum where this newly gathered community may ponder how the normative morality surrounding female virginity and sexuality shapes women's feelings, aspirations, experience in the world, and internal conflicts. In the garden, it is possible to dispute the social norms that justify violence against women and offer sympathy to the violator (Talattof 2000, 141–148). By speaking frankly about these matters in a voice easily heard, Parsipur demystifies sexuality, virginity, and the female body.

Another fascinating aspect of *Women Without Men* that encouraged the adventure of translation was Parsipur's pioneering struggle under pressure from state ideology and during a time of rapid change. Her success showed that women authors did not have to cower behind their veils leading lives of silence, that they did not have to accept an inactive and conscripted existence. Her work provided a prototype for a new generation of women writers who no longer wanted to be confined within the leftist, semi-Marxist literary discourse of the pre-revolutionary period, when socialist-realist authors, de-emphasizing form in favor of content, used a set of common metaphors to promote political change while demoting gender issues.

A measure of the degree of the book's universality is its reception. Upon its publication, *Women Without Men* received a tremendous amount of attention from readers and critics. When first published in Iran in its original language, the book became immediately popular and was the topic of discussion among intellectuals and literary communities. (The book was later published several times in the United States in Persian, where it sold out in a short while.) It was banned soon after publication, a fact that speaks to its importance as a voice of opposition. In Iran, the book was criticized at the time of its publication mostly for its naked language and perhaps for its uncovering taboos, and its revealing the body. It was considered an immoral work. Farzaneh Milani writes,

> It is hardly surprising that the most negative criticisms of her last popular novel, *Women Without Men,* revolve around the author's alleged unconcerned for *Sharm* [Shame]. "This book is written with total disregard for moral considerations and utter shamelessness [Bisharmi]," writes one critic. "The only art of this

> writer is her guts to say things that others have shame in expressing," complains another. (Milani 53)

The critics quoted by Milani obviously meant to discount the novel's author; however and ironically so, others applauded the author for her bravery and celebrated the work as a literary achievement in its own right. Indeed, Parsipur soon gained due respect and a prominent literary recognition across ideological lines.

The English translation has been reviewed positively by readers on the Internet and elsewhere who have praised it for a variety of reasons. The academic response to the book has been particularly forthcoming and positive. Nasrin Rahimieh writes,

> Certain segments of the novella are situated in 1953, while others are not clearly dated. This produces a sense of timelessness that obliges the reader to go beyond the image and condition of Iranian women in the post-revolutionary era. In fact, it insists that we grapple with deeply-rooted cultural attitudes that have long placed women in a place of social subordination. Parsipur's story depicts characters who wish to stand outside the dominant social conventions. But she also portrays characters whose lives are at the mercy of precepts

> that insist upon women's modesty, virginity, and obedience. Moreover, she presents us with female characters who themselves uphold and perpetuate these ideals of womanhood. (Rahimieh 2)

In recognizing the struggle of Iranian women, professors teaching courses related to Iranian and Middle Eastern women and gender issues frequently include *Women Without Men* on their syllabi. Since the English-language edition made its first appearance (the first of her works to be translated into any other language), the work has been translated into other languages as well. Moreover, several of Parsipur's other works have been translated with some acclaim into English, French, Italian, and German. We celebrate this extensive publication and recognition, which helps ensure that a broader audience of readers understands the context and content of this important book.

Kamran Talattof
Tuscon, Arizona
2003

WORKS CITED

Milani, Farzaneh. *Veils and Words: The Emerging Voices of Iranian Women Writers.* Syracuse: Syracuse University Press, 1992.

Rahimieh, Nasrin. "Shahrnush Parsipur, *Women Without Men: A Novella.*" *Iranian Studies* 33:1–2 (winter/spring 2000): 222–223.

Talattof, Kamran. "Iranian Women's Literature: From Pre-revolutionary Social Discourse to Postrevolutionary Feminism." *International Journal of Middle East Studies* 29:4 (Nov. 1997): 531–558.

———. *The Politics of Writing in Iran: A History of Modern Persian Literature.* Syracuse: Syracuse University Press, 2000.

Shahrnush Parsipur was born in Iran in 1946. She published her first short stories in literary magazines at the age of sixteen, and went on to write essays, story collections, and several novels. She was arrested for the first time in 1974, by the Shah's intelligence agency, and would be jailed three additional times under the Islamic Republic. While incarcerated she wrote the first part of her masterpiece *Touba and the Meaning of Night*, published by the Feminist Press in its first English-language edition in 2004. Now living and writing in exile in the United States, Parsipur is the first recipient of Brown University's International Writing Fellowship, designed to provide support for established creative writers who find it difficult to practice free expression in their home countries.

Kamran Talattof is associate professor of Persian literature and Iranian culture at the University of Arizona. He is the author, coauthor, or coeditor of many books, including *The Politics of Writing in Iran: A History of Modern Persian Literature*.

Jocelyn Sharlet is assistant professor of comparative literature at University of California, Davis. She specializes in Arabic language and literature, Persian literature, Turkish language, and Islamic civilization.

Persis M. Karim is assistant professor of English and comparative Literature at San Jose State University. A poet and writer, she is coauthor and coeditor of *A World Between: Poems, Short Stories, and Essays by Iranian-Americans* and editor of *Let Me Tell You Where I Have Been: New Writing by Women of the Iranian Diaspora*.

